MIAMI BEAT III

Illusions

Miami Beat III

Illusions

FREDERICA BURDEN

Contact: Frederica Burden
Email: miamibeat2017@gmail.com
Facebook Page: Miami Beat: The Secret Society

RCS Publishing, Leah G. Reynolds
Rcspublishingandmediagrp.com

Book Cover Design: Audria Wooster
Designbyindigo.com

Dedication

I would like to dedicate this book to the three men in my life who have always supported everything that I have done, and everything that I continue to do. Adam, Devin, and Davon, I love you to the moon and back with pit stops in between. Family forever over everything else.

Acknowledgements

I would first and always like to thank God for giving me this vision, and the ability to carry it out.

Thank you to all of the Miami Beat readers for requesting additional reading and keeping me on my toes to get it done, here it is!

This is the last of the trilogy, but not the last you will hear from the gang!!! Miami Beat has a lot more in store.

Leah Reynolds, our bond is unbreakable, and we have much more to offer our Secret Society...

Thanks to all that have supported me throughout my journey. It has been a joy bringing all of my characters out to meet all of you and sharing their stories.

Miami Beat III: Illusions is jaw dropping, and will tie everything together for you so sit back, relax, and as always, let the reading begin!

Prologue

"What the fuck?" Spencer screamed as he dropped the box on the floor and brought his hands to his face in fright. Artie wrapped his arms around Spencer and held him tight. Artie didn't know what to do; besides comfort Spencer. "Artie, what am I going to do to get out of this mess?" Spencer cried as Artie rubbed his shoulder. "Do you know who sent this to you? Do you know who's body part is in the box?" Artie demanded.

Spencer could only cry. He didn't respond to Artie.

Artie walked Spencer to the couch and helped him sit down. "Calm down, honey," he pleaded as Spencer wiped the tears from his cheeks. "Steven's going to kill me!" Spencer screamed. "I got you, don't worry," Artie said as he grabbed the box and tossed it into a large kitchen garbage bag. Spencer watched as Artie left the house with the bag and returned empty handed.

"I'm just going to check around the house. Just stay here. It will be okay. I promise," Artie coaxed as Spencer nodded his head in agreement. "Alright," Spencer said as Artie slowly backed out of the room. Suddenly a loud bang sounded from the back of his house. Spencer jumped as the noise grew louder. He and Artie both stared at each other. As if they were reading each other's minds. Artie and Spencer both ran towards the back door where the noise began to grow louder.

Artie ran into the room closest to the bathroom and came back holding his service weapon. Artie was determined to get to the bottom of this madness. He had to protect himself, and he had to protect Spencer. He looked over at Spencer. His handsome face was contorted into a scream, but nothing came out. "Don't worry," Artie said as he wrapped his arms around Spencer in a bear hug.

Spencer's heart skipped a beat as he watched his man in full "Rambo" mode.

Spencer leaned forward with his hand across his chest as Artie ran out of the house checking the perimeter of his house. Spencer tried to collect his thoughts as he prayed silently that Artie would return to him, in one piece. Every time Spencer closed his eyes, he saw Steven's sinister grin on the television. Steven sent him a direct threat. He promised Spencer that he would find him.

Spencer glanced in the floor where the box once sat. Steven was crazy enough to deliver a box with his dead wife's mouth in it. The entire thing was absolutely insane. One moment Spencer was enjoying the festivities at the parade and then the next moment he found himself in the middle of a crazy love triangle.

Spencer's hands shook as he tried to calm himself down. His mind kept drifting towards Steven and Linda. Linda's homely face remained etched in his brain. Steven was a great lay, but he wasn't worth Spencer's entire life. Steven was crazy enough to try and ruin Spencer or much worse, kill him. There was no hiding from him. Steven had a gruesome surprise package delivered to Spencer.

A terrible shiver ran up Spencer's spine. Steven was watching him. Now he had involved Artie in his mess. Spencer felt awful. Suddenly, Spencer heard Artie scream, "Stop!" and then he heard three gunshots. Spencer screamed and ran to the door. When he opened the door, he nearly fainted.

"Oh, my God!" Spencer screamed.

Chapter 1

Heavy drops of rain splattered across her windshield as she increased the speed of her wiper blades and boosted the volume on the radio. Vondra hummed along as Avant belted out the song, "Separated" in her ear. As she murmured along, she allowed her body actually to feel the lyrics.

If it weren't for her dear husband, she wouldn't be in her current situation. He made her behave in such a violent manner. If only he had been faithful and understanding, she wouldn't have had to resort to so many lengths.

Marcus Mystic had been her obsession since she met him. Vondra would never hurt him, although she considered it several times. She did have a plan about how she wanted to beat him. She could see Sidney's face as clear as day. Her long bouncy curls, smooth complexion, and enchanting smile clouded Vondra's entire mind. It infuriated Vondra that Sidney didn't understand what it meant to be with someone like Mystic. Loving him would destroy Sidney.

Vondra knew it. He would cheat on Sidney just like he cheated on her. Vondra was sure of it, and in her mind, she could already see it. Sidney's lovely face would surely change after the first time she caught Mystic staring longingly in the direction of another woman.

Vondra smiled at the thought then reconsidered it. She was actually thinking about another woman with her husband. That was the kind of control Sidney possessed.

"That Bitch thought that she was going to shake her ass in front of my husband and I would go out like some punk," Vondra mumbled to herself. "She'll be the first to go once I get my son," she said aloud. "The first to go," Vondra repeated as she considered how she would remove Sidney from the equation. She wanted to break Sidney's heart before she killed her. Then, Sidney would know what it felt like to have her spirit crushed, and Vondra would be able to witness it all.

As she considered the many options to end Sidney's existence, Vondra drove mindlessly. According to the GPS directions, her trip would take twenty hours, but she didn't care how long it would be. Vondra was ready to take what belonged to her or better yet, who belonged to her.

Once she returned home with their son, Mystic would have to fall back in line. If not, she would cause a substantial public nightmare for him, the last thing Mystic would want.

She glanced at her reflection in the mirror and cringed. Vondra decided that she would have to update her appearance before she returned home. Mystic wouldn't be able to resist her with a new makeover.

Vondra had a plan.

Mystic would be hers again, and their son would make them a complete family. For the first time, she would have exactly what she longed for. Vondra grinned sheepishly as she considered their bright future.

Mystic was now the Police Chief, and she couldn't wait to live the life of a Chief's wife. Vondra laughed to herself as she envisioned her new wardrobe and imagined how stunning she would look wearing Neiman's new fall line. "Ooh, yes," she coached as the images flashed in her mind rapidly.

Suddenly, the car in front of her slammed on brakes sending Vondra careening forward at 90 mph. As she snapped out of her dream, Vondra realized that the traffic had stalled considerably.

She stopped only inches away from the car in front of her. "Whew," she exhaled as her heart rate quickened in pace. Shaken but still determined, she took in a deep breath and let it out slowly. "Okay, Vondra you gotta chill and pay attention," she said reminding herself to stay in the present.

Vondra had her fair share of car accidents and fender benders due to daydreaming in the past. The last thing she needed was a car accident to derail her plans. Vondra saw the images of her son in her head as she drove along. "He probably looks just like his daddy right now," she cooed sweetly.

Vondra imagined that Lil' Marcus would be seven by now. She wondered how tall he was. Vondra knew that she would never be able to have children. It was confirmed the day her mother walked in on her father raping her.

That fateful day replayed in Vondra's mind often. Her mother screamed at the top of her lungs and charged at her father in anger. Vondra watched helplessly as her entire world crumbled, but sadly that wasn't the end of it. Vondra had to endure hours worth of questioning and medical exams in the Emergency Room.

She could still hear the dreadful stillness in the doctor's voice as he delivered the terrible news to her mother. She had been raped and molested repeatedly by her father. The rape caused a great deal of damage to Vondra's tiny body, especially her reproductive system.

Everything changed after that day.

Six months later, Vondra and her sister Elsa held hands while her father was sentenced to 35 years in prison for aggravated rape. That evening, unbeknownst to everyone, Vondra sentenced her mother to an execution. Vondra could still see the fear in her mother's eyes as she wrapped the elastic band around her mother's throat.

Something inside of Vondra snapped. Years of sexual abuse tainted her self-esteem and damaged her psyche. The doctor's news was the final straw. When she realized that she would never be able to have children, she thought of herself as worthless. Even as a young child, Vondra was aware of life's expectations. She was expected to have a good career, a husband, and most importantly, children.

Who would marry her if she couldn't have children?

Vondra blamed herself. She hated her existence. Every time she saw her reflection in the mirror, it made her angry. Seeing her mirrored image in Elsa made her furious.

In Vondra's opinion, it was all Elsa's fault. All of her troubles and her pain were because she protected her sister, Elsa. Vondra held on to the irrational belief and secretly seethed with hate towards her sister as a result.

Elsa noticed her sister's solemn behavior after the Emergency Room visit. When Vondra shared with her the ghastly details, the girls cried together. Elsa felt responsible for her sister's pain. Vondra gave up her chances of being a mother by protecting her sister. If Vondra hadn't sacrificed herself for Elsa's safety, it would have been Elsa suffering.

Vondra thought that she was protecting her twin sister by offering herself to her father instead. He promised to leave Elsa alone if she complied. The morning before Elsa and Vondra were shipped to their first of many foster homes, the girls made a deal.

"Since you gave yourself for me...I'll give you my first born child, Vondra," Elsa said holding her sister tightly. "You mean it?" Vondra asked with shock in her voice. "I know you'll find a husband if I help you have a baby," Elsa assured her sister with a proud smile. Vondra's eyes lit up at the promise her sister made. All of her fears were suddenly erased now that Elsa promised to help her.

She felt lucky to have Elsa.

"Pinky swear," Elsa promised as the girls locked pinky fingers and hugged tightly.

While the experience traumatized Vondra and her sister Elsa, both ladies managed to move forward with their lives. Elsa left for college and enrolled at the University of

Miami. It was on the palm tree-lined campus where she met Marcus Mystic. Her first love. Elsa couldn't hide her surprise the day Marcus approached her in the library.

"I've noticed you around campus. You're in the criminal justice program, right?" Marcus asked with mischievous curiosity. "Yes," Elsa responded with a sly grin. "So am I," he said with a nod. "Would you like to hang out sometime?" he asked her.

Elsa accepted his invitation, and the rest was history. Their passionate love affair was a steamy romance. They became best friends. Elsa didn't have many friends on campus besides her roommate Sara. An exchange student from Peru, Sara was Elsa's only confidant, but that was before she met Marcus.

Marcus filled all of her free time. He opened Elsa up to a whole new world, exposing her to Sun Tzu, "The Art of War" and the Law of Attraction. They spent time fantasizing about places that they couldn't pronounce being their homes. Elsa was sure that she had found the man who would marry her and complete the fairytale that she desperately clung to.

Her dreams were shattered when seven months after declaring their love for each other, Marcus dropped a bombshell on her. He told her that he was leaving college. Marcus could no longer afford his tuition at the University. Although the news devastated Elsa, she understood. If it weren't for scholarships and loans, she would never have gotten as far as she did.

Elsa and Marcus vowed to keep their love burning strong while he relocated to his Aunt's home, to find a job. "Don't worry, baby. Once I find a job and can save some money we will find a place and make this work," Marcus assured Elsa. She tried to contain her tears as she watched her lover disappear into the night on the two-hour drive back home. Though she would never admit it, Elsa was inconsolable for the first week they spent apart. Her roommate Sara was her only saving life force.

Marcus and Elsa kept their pledge for a few months while Marcus searched for a job. The couple endured several months apart before Marcus decided to call Elsa, preparing to give up. The job hunt didn't go as well as Marcus expected, initially, but he continued searching. Elsa consoled Marcus and tried to assure him that his dream job was on the horizon. She was right!

Marcus called Elsa bubbling with excitement. He could barely contain himself when he announced that he had been accepted into the Police Academy in Miami.

Elsa congratulated her man and vowed her support. She would stand by him as he underwent the rigors of the Police Academy process. Elsa's workload and lack of transportation made it difficult to make the time to see Marcus. It wouldn't have done her any good, however.

The physical and academic strictness of the Academy forced Marcus to cancel many of their plans. Elsa was saddened, but she pressed on. Elsa knew that soon Marcus would be a Police Officer and they would live together in the town where he was employed. They talked on the phone daily. When they did spend time together, she made sure that it was extra special.

Elsa couldn't contain her excitement when Marcus called her out of the blue to tell her that he was heading to see her. To her surprise, he was coming to take her to dinner.

Things in the Academy were progressing along well, and Marcus had been hinting about searching for a home outside of Miami. Elsa just knew it in her heart that he was going to propose to her over dinner. She couldn't wait to tell him that she was carrying their baby.

Elsa imagined the joy that he would feel when she told him the news. They met at the Ohho Noodles Market in Coral Gables for dinner. Marcus was already sitting at the table when she arrived. He stood the minute he saw her and wrapped his strong arms around her body.

They both began talking excitedly. Elsa told him, "you first," excited about her burgeoning belly. She figured that she would tell him about the baby after he proposed. Taking in a deep breath, Marcus gathered Elsa's hands in his and stared into her eyes.

He said, "I came here to tell you...you know...that I am in the Police Academy. It's a lot of hard work, and a great deal is expected of me. I don't see where we can make this work. I tried, and I can't commute back and forth. The traffic is horrific, and it's too much on me. We never see each other. I have study group on the weekend. These next six months will be hard on us, and I don't want to keep you from living your life," he said.

Elsa looked into his eyes, lost, and fighting back the tears. "Now, what do you want to tell me?" Marcus asked curiously. "You beat me to it, I was thinking the same thing," she said sadly letting go of his hand. That evening Elsa listened to Marcus talk about the Police Academy and his new future. A future that didn't include her.

Marcus held her tightly and kissed her for the last time. Elsa walked towards her dorm without bothering to look back. Just as he planned, Marcus Mystic continued with the Police Academy and graduated at the top of his class. Elsa dropped out of school without completing her junior year.

Vondra's demons continued to chase her which forced her to visit a therapist. Vondra gained the medications to help keep the voices and negativity at bay. The therapists and heavy doses of Klonopin helped her tremendously. Vondra was able to pursue higher education and put her focus into a career in nursing.

Vondra applied and was accepted to Miami Dade Community College Medical Campus to further her education in nursing. The prestigious college was Vondra's first choice because successful graduates were guaranteed positions at the nearby Ryder Trauma Center.

Professionally, she was doing well. Vondra obtained a position in her field soon after graduation. She still thought about her sister, but her thoughts changed. She needed to show Elsa that she could find someone to love her.

Vondra dated but was dissatisfied with the selection of available men. She could find plenty of men who wanted to sleep with her, but no one wanted anything after that. After several restraining orders, and a few slashed tires, Vondra began to give up on dating entirely. No one wanted Vondra's heart.

Emotionally, Vondra felt dead inside.

It wasn't until Marcus Mystic entered the picture that things took a sharp turn. Vondra worked as a nurse in the local hospital. In her position, she saw law enforcement regularly. Marcus Mystic stood out to her. It was his charm, his charisma; and the bulge she noticed inside his pants the day she helped clean his wound.

She instantly fell for the handsome Police Major. It wasn't until she had an opportunity to talk to him that she realized that there was a problem. Major Mystic looked right at Vondra and smiled brightly. "Elsa? Elsa is that you?" he asked as she stared at him in surprise.

She continued dressing Mystic's wound as she considered her options.

Vondra was used to being mistaken for her sister, but she never heard Elsa's name mentioned at the hospital. Elsa wasn't a nurse. Vondra was also sporting a short haircut. She never knew her sister to wear her hair above shoulder length. She wondered how Mystic knew her sister. Vondra smiled at the handsome man and shook her head. "No, my name is Vondra," she said shyly.

"You remind me so much of...someone. Someone who got away," he said with a frown as Vondra considered his statement. "Do you know someone named Elsa?" he asked with hopeful anticipation in his voice. "No," Vondra said quickly. Mystic's question about Elsa intrigued Vondra.

Vondra and Mystic became inseparable from that moment forward. Every second that Vondra spent with

Mystic she wondered how Mystic knew Elsa, and why his eyes lit up when he called her name.

She began to fake pregnancy symptoms in a ploy to trick Mystic into a quick marriage. When Mystic put the small diamond on Vondra's finger, she was ecstatic. Vondra tracked her sister down to let her know that she had found the man to start her family with, that she was getting married.

Elsa welcomed her sister into her small apartment with open arms. The two sisters embraced warmly as they both tried to block the painful memories that their union induced.

"You have a nice place," Vondra complimented as she looked around her sister's modest home. It was decorated nicely with bright yellow walls. As the two women filled each other in on their lives, Vondra's mind drifted to their childhood. "I'm getting married sis," Vondra said wearing a proud grin as her sister's mouth dropped in surprise.

"That's terrific, sis!" Elsa said with glee.

In the distance, she heard the whine of a baby's cry and jumped. "Who was that?" Vondra asked startled. Elsa laughed heartily and gave her sister a reassuring pat on the shoulder. "That was your nephew," Elsa laughed disappearing into the hallway to retrieve the baby.

When she returned she was carrying the sweetest chubby-cheeked baby, Vondra had ever seen. His bright eyes twinkled as he grinned at his aunt. Vondra reached out to take him, holding the baby close to her chest.

"I didn't know you had a baby," Vondra gushed recalling the pinky promise that she shared with her sister many years prior. "Yes, he's my little angel," Elsa said with a proud smile. "His name is Marcus. Marcus, Jr. He looks just like his father", Elsa said.

Vondra took note of the baby's bright green eyes and smiled lovingly at him. "You know, sis, being in the medical field you find out interesting stuff. Since we're identical twins. Marcus is not only my nephew but my son as well," Vondra said with a laugh. "Since we share the same DNA," Vondra added as she held Marcus tightly in her arms. The little toddler grinned at Vondra, confused by her striking resemblance to his mother.

Elsa was startled by Vondra's admission. Clasping her hands together she let out a deep breath and made an attempt to change the subject. "So, you're getting married?" Elsa asked as her sister nodded proudly displaying her ring. "Who is he?" she asked.

"I call him Mystic, but his first name is Marcus," Vondra said with a grin. "We met in the hospital where I work," she said as her sister gasped in surprise. "What?" Elsa stammered. "I know Marcus!" Elsa whispered in shock. "Marcus is his father," Elsa said pointing at the baby in Vondra's arms.

Vondra stared at the baby, taking in his appearance; his eyes were green and sparkled with excitement. He was an adorable little baby, and she was already in love with him.

Vondra turned the ring on her finger nervously. The moment she saw little Marcus, she knew that he belonged to her. She didn't want to give him back to her sister.

Elsa watched her sister's reaction when she introduced her baby recalling the promise she made long ago. Her son was the only attachment she had of her time with Mystic. The greatest love Elsa had ever experienced. Watching her son smile playfully in her sister's arms, Elsa saw a miniature version of the one man she truly loved, Marcus Mystic.

Elsa shook her head in despair. "Marcus and I met at U of M. We fell in love, or so I thought it was," Elsa said sadly. "He had to leave college, and that's when things fell apart for us," Elsa explained. "Marcus ended our relationship. He said that the lack of time and distance was too much for him," Elsa said as Vondra hugged her sister.

"Wow, sis. If only I had known that he knew you first, I would have never dealt with him," Vondra lied. The truth was, Vondra enjoyed chasing after Elsa's boyfriends; aspiring to prove that she was the most desired twin. The fact that Marcus Mystic chose to marry her and not Elsa was the sweetest revenge, ever.

Elsa was broken inside, but she refused to let it show. The man she loved was about to marry her sister. Overtaken by despair and heartache, Elsa couldn't bring herself to attend her sister's wedding. Elsa opted instead to stay out of her sister's life, and renege on her pinky promise, or so she thought.

Vondra, on the other hand, had different plans. She was determined to be a mother. After she and Marcus married,

Vondra put her plan into action. She vowed to complete her family one day. All she needed was her son, Marcus.

"Soon everything will be perfect, again," she whispered to herself as the GPS instructed her to continue on her charted route.

"I'll see you soon, sis," Vondra declared as she pressed her foot on the gas and roared down the highway in the direction of her dreams.

The flashback of Elsa and Vondra hugging and giving each other a pinky promise for Elsa to give her sister her first born became much clearer in Vondra's mind.

Chapter 2

Arnold Billingsley III 's head swung from one side of the room to the other as he made sure to catch the full chaotic scene that unfolded in front of him. Sidney watched in horror as the tall, burly guard dragged her brother out of the visiting area, howling threats at him.

She shot Mystic a questioning look as he glared at his feet in response. Sidney wanted to scream at the top of her lungs, but instead, she merely turned to face Arnold Billingsley III. "So, you will take my brother's case, right?" she confirmed as he nodded his head in agreement.

"I will make sure that your brother gets the justice he deserves, Ma'am," Arnold responded with a firm hand-shake. "Now, if you both would excuse me, I have to get back to my office," he said as he gave Mystic a handshake and walked out of the building.

Sidney didn't know what to do. She wanted to see if there was a way she could see her brother before she left for Miami.

She walked towards the receptionist area and took note of the sad frown the woman was wearing. "May I help you?" she asked as Sidney responded, "Yes, I was wondering if I would be able to see my brother later today," she asked as the receptionist responded with a question, "Name?" she asked.

"Randy Stevens, Jr.," Sidney responded hopefully as the receptionist's fingers moved across the computer keys, swiftly. "I'm sorry. He's on lockdown for the remainder of the day. Visiting hours start at 9 tomorrow morning," she said. Sidney thanked her and turned to leave the building, that was when she noticed him.

Mystic stood off to the side of the receptionist area. He no longer appeared to be the robust and formidable force that she knew him to be. For some reason, he looked weak to Sidney. There was something about him that made her want to run to him and wrap her arms around him, then she remembered what her brother said, and it made her want to punch him.

She thought about the night of passion they shared together. She would never have slept with him had she known about his history.

She tried to calm her racing thoughts. Sidney fought against her emotions, challenging herself to not fall apart inside the Police Precinct. She needed the sanctity of her own room to completely collapse in tears like she genuinely desired.

As a lonely tear traveled down her cheek, she quickly swiped it away and walked swiftly out of the building without saying a word to Mystic. She didn't turn around to see if he followed behind her. At that point, it didn't matter to Sidney. Her brother told her all that she needed to know.

Sidney had to believe Randy, Jr. right? Why would he lie about who he saw that night? Sidney saw the visions from that fateful evening, every single time she closed her eyes at night. She knew that her brother didn't make anything up. She was sure that he had the same nightmares that she experienced.

She waited until Mystic used the remote to unlock the car doors without looking back at him. Sidney was so angry she could spit. Sidney slammed the door and let out a sigh. It was all over. Her fairytale; everything that she planned for herself and Mystic was all over. She couldn't be with him if he were involved in the murder of her father.

When Mystic opened the car door and sat down, Sidney didn't turn to face him. She could feel his eyes burrowing into her. It felt like he was trying to see her soul. Sidney feared that if he saw it, he would run. She was so hurt and heartbroken. The first man Sidney gave herself to was involved in her father's murder. She hoped that it was all a mistake. Mystic was the only man she ever loved. The fear of losing what she thought she wanted most, devastated her.

Mystic cleared his throat, but Sidney didn't react. He coughed loudly, and she pretended as if he didn't make a sound. Sidney acted as if she were in the car alone. For the first time in a long time, she wished that she were alone. "Sidney, I love you so much. You are the most important person in my life," he pleaded as he stared into her eyes, lovingly.

"Please, Sidney," he begged. "Please, say something!" as hot tears slid down his face and his voice cracked. Sidney couldn't believe it, he was crying.

Ordinarily, his tears would have melted Sidney's heart, but something stopped her from seeing the pain in his words. While his tears seemed genuine, Sidney couldn't get the image of her brother's face out of her mind. Randy Jr. meant precisely what he said when he saw Mystic. He wouldn't have made anything up like that, especially while he was facing a murder charge.

"What the fuck was that all about?" she demanded.

Chapter 3

Florence Stevens kneeled on the soft prayer rug and began her prayers for the day. She prayed over each of her three children, Sidney, Randy Jr., and Cero. Although none of them were babies, they still took so much of her mental energy. Florence was a Christian woman, but she was also aware of the ways the world could ruin a person.

She worried about her children.

Drugs, pain, and chaos were all things that she knew too well. They all surrounded her in the community where she lived. Florence was a hard working, God fearing woman, but life wasn't easy for her. She never expected it to be. Florence knew that she would have to work twice as hard in her life to gain the things that she wanted and needed. She and Randy Sr. were heading in the direction of obtaining the American Dream.

Florence still dreamed about the night she lost it all. Memories of that night kept her awake. She couldn't shake the image of Randy Sr. being carried out by the Cops from her mind. A devout Christian and a dedicated mother, Florence spent every waking moment with her children. They were her everything.

She worked double shifts to provide for her children after Randy Sr. was murdered. Florence didn't care what it took; she was determined to show her children a better life. As Florence glanced out her tiny kitchen window, she groaned. The Dope Boys were already working, and it was only 9:00 am. She watched as the young men passed their toxic product from one person to the next.

It was so upsetting to Florence. The entire neighborhood was overwrought with drugs and crime. The degradation of her neighborhood weighed heavily on her heart. "Dear God, I know that you are a healer and a deliverer. God, I ask that today you come into this house and soothe our spirits. I also ask that you keep your hands upon each one of my children, Lord. You know where they are and what they're doing. Even when I don't," she said as she ended her prayer with a sincere, "Amen."

"Amen," she heard from the corner of the room. Florence jumped at the sound and then smiled at her son Cero. He was growing into a handsome young man. The more he matured, however, the more afraid Florence became. She loved her son, desperately, but she knew that soon she wouldn't be able to handle his outbursts.

Cero was already taller than her at 16 years of age. It was all too much for her to bear, but Florence never complained. Every day she arose from bed and took care of her son with the same loving kindness that she did with her other children. She would never admit that it was all beginning to wear her down.

He was a good boy most of the time, but Autism is a Spectrum Disorder that affected his moods, behavior, and communication. She understood that Cero's limitations didn't make his ability to handle disappointments and frustrations well, but she tried her best to teach him.

Florence's latest exasperation was with Cero's behavior at school. Florence prayed that one day her son would find his way inside a great school and community where he can meet friends and learn to manage his moods effectively.

She knew that such a place existed; it just was never within her price range, until now. Florence was grateful that the checks she received hadn't ceased, she just needed to do a little more research. She needed the money, and it was always right on time. She prayed that Sidney would never have to return to a cold or dark home, again.

Florence was proud of all of her children, but she had the highest hopes in her daughter Sidney. Sidney vowed to take care of her mother forever. At first, Florence thought that the checks were coming from Sidney, but once she saw the look on her daughter's face as she examined one of them, Florence realized that she knew nothing about the checks.

Chapter 4

The scream of someone being tased rang out in the air causing everyone to jump and stand at attention. Randy Jr. looked around the room and tried to hold in his fear. No matter what he felt, he had to keep himself together and maintain the façade. It was all a game, not a fun game, but a game nevertheless. He had to maintain a poker face, no matter what went down in there.

He could hear the screams and chants coming from the room before the guards unlocked the door. There was some commotion going on on the floor above him, and by the looks of things, someone was going to end up dead. That was life on the inside.

Randy Jr. was still reeling from seeing Mystic from earlier. He was so pissed he wanted to rip his head off, but he couldn't reach him. In fact, he was drug out of there before he could jump on him and beat his ass like he wanted to do. It killed Randy Jr. to be inside the prison.

He hated being in there.

It had been nearly two weeks, but it felt like he had been in there for two months. His mind drifted back to the fat ass attorney and his solution to Randy Jr.'s regretful set of circumstances. Based on the charges they were trying to pin on him, he stood a chance at a life sentence in a maximum-security prison. Currently, he was staying in a low-security area, but he knew that it was only a matter of time before he would be transferred.

It pissed him off that he was being charged with Sunshine's murder. He would never harm a woman. As good as his mother was to him, it hurt Randy Jr. to consider how she would react to his incarceration. She made him promise her that he would not return to prison and here he was less than three years later, back at square one.

Randy Jr. felt hopeless. He knew that he had to find a way out of the situation he was in. Randy Jr. watched as the guards dragged four inmates from their cells to the hole. He breathed a sigh of relief as the guards tossed him into his cell and closed the hard, metal door shut. Randy Jr. was just grateful that they didn't beat him down for his behavior in the visitor's lounge. He knew that he would face repercussions for trying to fight the guard who held him back.

He later explained to the guard that it wasn't personal. He was just trying to get that Cop Fucker. Randy Jr. was infuriated by the smug expression on his punk ass face. It took everything in him not to gouge Mystic's eyes out. Randy Jr. also noticed the attraction between his sister and that cop. He prayed that his sister wasn't stupid enough to ignore what he told her.

Randy Jr. had no questions about his memory. He knew exactly what every cop in that house looked like. He remembered their faces. It was etched in his brain.

The night he lost his father, he lost everything; his role model, his best friend, and his confidant. Randy Sr. was the James Evans, the dad of the that old 70's show, Good Times, in their family. He loved his children, and he was a disciplinarian, but most importantly he was always there for them.

When his father was murdered, Randy Jr. watched his entire life unravel at the age of 19. He loved his father, and he knew that one day he would be able to avenge Randy Sr.'s murder. One day he would make things right.

First, he had to figure his way out of his current dilemma.

Chapter 5

Vera held the phone in her trembling hand, praying that this time, she would receive an answer. The North Florida Mental Hospital was teaming with Police Officers, Detectives, and Investigators, not to mention dealing with terrified patients. Vera was trying to reach her nephew but to no avail. It seemed like as soon as Marcus dropped his wife off at the hospital, he completely disappeared.

It infuriated Vera. She knew that the poor woman had mental issues and Vondra was a public threat to everyone in Florida and the surrounding states, but she was also a human.

The longer her nephew ignored her calls, the more Vera considered Vondra's words about her husband. Vondra often commented that her husband loved her. She truly believed that Marcus was planning to return to retrieve her. Although her delusions sounded unfounded, Vera wondered if Vondra had already reached Marcus and hatched her plan of vengeance.

When Vondra escaped from the hospital, she left a trail of blood and bodies. Vera shuddered to consider what would happen the longer Vondra remained loose. Her nephew was in danger, but he was too foolish to answer his phone.

She knew in her heart that he was ignoring her. That was Marcus' way. He preferred to stick his head in the sand as opposed to dealing with his troubles head-on. It was such a frustrating thing for Vera, but she loved Marcus enough to overlook his shortcomings. Vera was just worried that Vondra would hurt him.

After talking to Elsa, Vondra's twin sister, on the phone that day, Vera grew more terrified of her escaped patient. She hadn't slept soundly since Vondra's escape. She kept seeing Lawrence's face in her head. The way his eyes looked like he knew what was happening would be the end. The way his mouth looked like he was smiling peacefully at Vera. She screamed in horror when she found his body.

The therapists and doctors on staff urged Vera to take some time off, but she just could not. Vera's entire life was tied into North Florida Mental Hospital. If she left, the place would surely crumble. Vera considered the thought as she scratched at the chipped nail polish hanging on the tip of her right index finger. It was a nervous habit that she had picked up since the murders.

North Florida Mental Hospital had never experienced anything like what Vondra rained upon them. All of the patients were in an uproar. They were terrified that Vondra would return and kill them all. The therapists conducted regular sessions to help their most affected patients deal with the fear of Vondra's return.

Vera chuckled.

Never had they experienced a patient frightening enough to warrant the precautions that they had to put in place in case of Vondra's return. Everyone knew that she would be back there, they just didn't know who would be next to die.

As Vera redialed Mystic's cell phone number, she prayed that he wasn't next on Vondra's list.

Chapter 6

Lucy held the rosary beads in her hands as she completed her prayer. Every day she prayed for her grandson, Raoul. Lucy missed her baby every minute that he was away from her. The thought of Raoul locked away in the hellish prison made her skin crawl.

She needed her grandson in her life. Who else would be there with her when she felt lost and alone? Raoul was her lifeline and the reason why she arose every day to fight her demons.

If it weren't for his love, Lucy would have given up long ago.

Lucy struggled with depression, anxiety and several other mental issues that she chose to hold close to her chest. She took a daily regimen of prescription medications including lithium to help manage her symptoms.

She groaned at the memory of her beloved, Raoul stretched out in the hospital bed. Her heart broke slowly as she listened to her grandson recall the events that led him to the hospital.

A group of men attacked her grandson. They would've killed him if someone hadn't stepped in. Raoul saw the man who helped him as his hero. This man protected his life and threatened Raoul's attackers with certain death if they ever touched Raoul again.

She wept as she recalled her grandson's voice as he excitedly proclaimed. "That's him, Nana," her grandson called out motioning towards Tulea. Her heart sank when her eyes met Tulea's. Lucy was happy that he saved her baby from harm, but she couldn't risk Raoul and Tulea linking up together.

Tulea was not a good guy by any stretch of the imagination. His arrest record was quite lengthy, and it stemmed back as far as his childhood. Tulea was in trouble from adolescence, spending the majority of his life behind bars. He was the very last person Lucy wanted to be in contact with Raoul.

Lucy was aggravated that after all of her hard work and dedication towards raising Raoul into young adult-hood, he still ended up heading down the wrong path. She couldn't risk Tulea making matters worse. Raoul had a look of awe on his face when he saw Tulea. Lucy wondered how much longer she could keep the secret that Tulea was his father. She had to get him out of that prison before he learned the truth. Most importantly, he had to get out of the prison before Tulea had a chance to teach his son the ropes.

Lucy knew that prison was not all about rehabilitation. It was also an academic setting for those who wanted to become real criminals. Most people entered prison with the hopes of never returning. She wanted to make sure that Raoul hated his experience in prison enough to never return.

Chapter 7

The air in the Black Chevrolet Tahoe was thick enough to cut with a knife. Neither Sidney nor Mystic said a word to each other. In fact, he refused to say a word after her outburst. He just told her that they needed to discuss this once they were both calm. Sidney considered her options as she stared out the window. She could call him out and ask for an explanation about what her brother exposed, or she could wait.

Arguing with Mystic would have been futile. He wasn't the type of man who squabbled. Sidney was aware of Mystic's demeanor, he showed her that side of him several times before. Mystic didn't let his emotions show. Instead, he chose to keep it all locked inside behind a stone face.

Mystic drove down the highway in a hurry to reach their destination. He had plans for the evening, and they were all ruined after Randy Jr.'s accusation. He applied more pressure to his right foot, accelerating the vehicle beyond 70 mph. Mystic wanted to do something to show Sidney that her brother had it all wrong, but he knew that there was no way to do it. She would never believe him over her own brother.

Her face dissolved into deep sadness the minute she saw her brother in chains and prison orange. Sidney loved Randy Jr. more than anyone. Mystic looked over at her in the seat and wanted to wrap his arms around her.

He could tell that she was holding in her tears, afraid to let him see that vulnerable side of her again. In just that short amount of time, Sidney cut herself off entirely to him. Only 24 hours ago she lay naked in his arms, now she was hundreds of miles away from him.

The soft jazz music belting from the radio was interrupted as his cell phone rang for what seemed like the thousandth time. Mystic merely let the call ring until the caller gave up. Mystic was aware of who was trying to get in contact with him. He didn't have to look at his phone. His wife had been trying to reach him since he dropped her off at the mental institution.

Mystic couldn't catch a break at the moment. Mystic rubbed his hands over his face, feeling stubble underneath his hands and groaned. How could his dreams all come true and a day and a half later, his life is falling apart at the seams? He just didn't understand it. He had the girl, the Chief of Police position and the clout but now he was about to lose it all.

His wife, Vondra was on the warpath, determined to see him lose everything.

Mystic tried to fight, he struggled to hold on, but he felt that he was slowly losing his grip on everything that he held dear. He wanted to just run away and start over somewhere else, but even that was impossible. As the Chief of Police, his whereabouts had to be known.

He didn't mind the responsibilities of his job. This was all that he wanted, at the moment. Now, he just wanted silence.

Sadly, that was all Sidney was giving him.

He considered his next words. Mystic didn't want to get into anything in the car with Sidney. Before he could begin to explain anything to her, he needed to be able to hold both of her hands in his and look her in the eyes. She had to see that Mystic meant every word he spoke when he told her that he had nothing to do with her father's death.

Nearly twenty years, he worked hard to maintain a stellar professional image. Now, this punk Randy Jr. just leveled accusations at him that could cost him his current standing in the community.

Just the thought of him losing it all to that fiasco caused him to grit his teeth in frustration.

Randy Jr.'s outburst in the prison visitor's room nearly cost him everything. Mystic wanted to throat punch Randy Jr. when he lunged forward to fight him. Randy wanted to kick his ass and show him what a real beating felt like, but he couldn't do such a thing and defend his actions to Sidney. She would have hated him forever.

Mystic just had to find a way to convince Sidney he wasn't lying and to regain her trust.

Chapter 8

Sidney played with her hair absentmindedly as she considered her next move. She and Mystic had been riding in complete silence for nearly two hours. Sidney could feel the tension in her shoulders and back.

One minute she was in the arms of her beloved. She was floating on air knowing that she and Mystic shared a night of pure pleasure and love. She awoke that morning more in love with Mystic than she had ever felt.

Now, things were different. Randy Jr. exposed her new love to be someone she didn't know. The longer Mystic drove, the more Sidney considered her situation. Sidney was a planner and a plotter. If she could come up with an analytical approach to determining the truth, she would take it as opposed to the emotional one.

Mystic would completely shut down if she got too emotional on him. Sidney knew how men operated. She has two brothers. Neither of them could handle her emotions or her tears. Sidney figured if she broke down crying on Mystic, he would only clam up. She had to find a way to confront him with irrefutable facts. That way he would have no choice but to respond.

The minute the thought of her brothers crossed her mind Sidney had to resist the urge to cry. She missed Cero and Randy Jr. Sidney could only imagine what her mother was thinking at the moment. Just then her phone vibrated in her hands.

She glanced down at her phone and stifled the urge to answer her mother's call. Sidney felt terrible ignoring her mother, but she knew that she couldn't answer the barrage of questions that would be hurled her way.

Her mother hadn't spoken to either of her oldest children in days. For a mother like Florence, Sidney was sure it hurt worse than any physical pain to fear that your children were in harm's way. Sidney couldn't tell her mother where she was. If Florence Stevens knew that her daughter was in Georgia, she would want to know why. The minute Sidney told her mother about Randy Jr., Florence would completely lose her mind.

Randy Jr. wasn't a difficult child, but he found a way into mischief every chance he could. He didn't realize it, but his behavior had taken a toll on their family. They already had to manage Cero and his meltdowns, Randy Jr. made things so much more difficult for their family. Sidney tried to explain that exact position to her brother at one time. Randy Jr. didn't want to hear a word of advice from his sister.

He still blamed his dysfunction on their father's murder. Sidney loved her brother, but she didn't buy into the whole idea that since her father was no longer with them, she should give up.

She couldn't understand her brother, but she still sympathized with him. He was the reason why she didn't have to worry about anything growing up. Her brother always had her back. Any bully she ever faced turned into a quick acquaintance after they came across Randy Jr. He was her protector.

She was obligated to protect her brother Randy Jr. while he was helpless in prison. If she didn't do it, who would? Sidney accessed her Bank of America app on her cell phone and groaned when the balance appeared. She had much less money than she thought in her checking account.

She hadn't worked full-time since she entered the FBI Academy. During her time in the Academy, she didn't receive an income for her participation in the program. It caused a financial strain on her, but Sidney didn't complain. It was for her lifelong goal, so the temporary discomfort was expected.

Now that she had to spend money on her brother's attorney, Sidney questioned how much longer she would be able to get by without informing her mother. Sidney thought about the money that she found in Randy Jr.'s safe. She had to use it, or she would need Florence's financial assistance to help her pay for his defense, and she couldn't do that. The thought of adding more stress on her mother's shoulders frightened Sidney.

She couldn't lose her mother. The entire ordeal made her want to cry, but as angry as she felt towards Mystic she didn't want to cry in front of him. Mystic would comfort her if she got emotional and Sidney wasn't sure that she could handle his touch at the moment.

Sidney counted down the minutes until she would be safely inside her room. She had to check out the folder that Garcia gave her. This would answer her question without asking Mystic anything.

Somehow her fairytale existence suddenly turned on its ear.

She glanced over at Mystic. The sunlight hit his face, and it looked like he was covered in honey. She wanted to kiss him and have him tell her that everything would be alright. Sidney wanted Mystic to vehemently deny being in the same vicinity as her father that night. She wanted to hear that her brother had it all wrong.

Sidney wanted to hear anything other than the radio, and the road noise as Mystic roared down I 95. "Sidney would you like to get something to eat?" he asked as her heart leaped for joy. Sidney was starving, but she ignored her rumbling stomach and pursed her lips in frustration. "No, I'm fine," she responded as Mystic chuckled trying to lighten the mood.

"Are you sure?" he asked as he pulled off the road and turned into the Chick-fil-a drive-thru.

Sidney ordered her food, and they ate in silence. Sidney thought about her brother Randy Jr. and shivered. "Are you cold?" Mystic asked as he turned the air conditioner off. "No," she responded. "Sidney, your brother is mistaken. I don't want you to think that I'm some kind of monster. I am not. I love what I do, and most importantly,

I love you. I would never harm another person," he said facing her with pleading eyes.

Sidney stared deep into his green eyes as they misted over. "I would never hurt you," he reminded her as he softly kissed her lips. "I love you, Sidney," he said as he wrapped his arms around her.

Mystic was about to continue, but his cell phone interrupted him again. Glancing down at his phone he groaned in frustration. His office ringed him at the worst possible time.

Sidney's mind drifted between the substantial amount of cash in her suitcase and an uncomfortable journey home. She glanced at Mystic, his handsome jaw was clenched tight as he tried to ignore his phone ringing. She knew that things would never be the same for either of them.

The ride down I 95 towards Miami was a quiet and tense one. They both pretended to be more interested in the scenery along the route.

The minute Mystic pulled the car into the parking lot at the Police Station next to Sidney's car, she nearly jumped out of the passenger seat before he stopped. Sidney couldn't wait to put distance between her and Mystic. "Sidney, wait a minute," Mystic said sadly as she hopped out of the car and slammed the door.

Although her mind told her not to, she turned around and faced his distraught expression. "I love you," he said as she slammed the door closed. Sidney opened her car door and climbed inside the driver's seat, tossing the folder on the seat beside her. Sidney was glad that she closed the door before Mystic could say another word.

She wanted to cry, but Sidney refused to let him see her upset.

Instead, Sidney put the key in the ignition and turned the volume on the radio up loud. Ella Mai's latest tune belted from her speakers as she put the car in reverse and backed out of the parking space.

When she turned forward, as she put the car in drive, her eyes fell on the folder resting on the passenger seat. Suddenly, as she drove home, the floodgates opened, and the tears began to flow.

Chapter 9

The hard metal prison door slowly opened, sending a loud metal clanking sound throughout the facility. His unit was open for recreation time. It had been nearly two months since he was locked inside his cell and he felt like he was going to lose his mind.

The metal doors were his biggest annoyance. They were his sign of lost freedom. Randy Jr. tried his best to get used to the sound, but it still affected him.

Nighttime was the loneliest time for Randy Jr. This was the time when his mind raced with negative thoughts. He rarely slept at night. There was always drama or chaos occurring. The fact that he shared close living quarters with nearly 200 men made Randy Jr. uneasy enough to sleep with one eye open.

He had already been in two fights since he arrived at the prison. It didn't bother him, though. Randy Jr. was a fighter, and he was taught to hold his own.

His issue was sleep deprivation. Randy Jr. found it difficult to relax long enough to allow his body an opportunity for sleep. Things popped off at night, and some inmates didn't make it out alive. Since Randy Jr. arrived in the complex three men were sent to the infirmary for injuries sustained in their cells by their cellmates.

Randy Jr. didn't trust anyone in the prison. His cellmate Ray Wilson was a three-time convicted felon serving a life sentence for murder. Since Ray occupied the cell long before Randy Jr. arrived, Ray took control over the sleeping arrangements. He slept on the bottom bunk, and Randy Jr. rested on top.

Randy Jr. didn't mind as long as Ray didn't try any funny stuff with him. He knew that some of the other inmates didn't mind engaging in sexual activity with their cellmates, but Randy Jr. didn't mess with men in any capacity. He didn't judge the guys who did, however.

He understood how lonely a man could get in a tiny prison cell for 23 hours of their life, per day. He knew what the temptations in prison could be, but it didn't entice him.

He was grateful to see that his cellmate didn't swing in that manner either. It made for a more peaceful living arrangement since he didn't have to watch his back in that way, but that didn't mean Randy Jr. let his guard down. He never turned his back on anyone within the prison, guard or inmate.

He knew that the guards in the prison were dirtier than the inmates. They were underpaid, underappreciated, and sent inside a place where they had power and control. During the day the guards worked on duty, and at night the guards slept on duty.

Their only goal was to prevent chaos or melee on the floors. They could care less if someone was being abused or raped in their cells. The guards rarely protected inmates from each other. They just merely carted the injured inmates out of their cells when necessary.

When he first arrived at the prison, Randy Jr. believed that the prison had their own paramedics, because he saw them every day. Another prisoner later informed him that the paramedics were called daily to attend to inmates and guards. The prison was complete hell, and Randy Jr. was plotting on how he could get out.

He could hear the other inmates screaming and banging on their cell doors. Randy Jr. laid down on the lumpy mattress that was strewn over a set of metal slats. He hadn't had a comfortable sleep in months, and it was beginning to show. The food was horrible and moldy. If it weren't for his commissary, Randy Jr. would have been completely lost.

There were two things that Randy Jr. needed to survive, money and pussy. He made sure to keep a surplus of both around him at all times. Prison had a shortage of both, but Randy Jr. was still able to make due. He owed it all to Raine. Raine Thomas was a night guard at the prison and Randy Jr.'s new love interest. When the lights went out, Randy Jr. made hot passionate love to Raine.

Raine was a short woman with long, brunette hair and stark brown eyes that she kept hidden behind thick wire-framed glasses. She weighed over 200 pounds and always had a bright smile on her face. She wasn't pretty and was severely overweight, but Randy Jr. didn't complain. In fact, he sought Raine out. She was the first one to fall under his seductive spell.

He began his seductive dance by complimenting Raine's beautiful smile. Randy Jr. noticed that she would blush slightly when he complimented her. She was a bashful woman with a timid voice.

It confused Randy Jr. how Raine became a Correctional Officer with such diminutive qualities. He could tell by the way she smiled when he complimented her that she wasn't used to male attention.

Luckily for Randy Jr., this was his specialty. He had the ability to make any woman feel like the sexiest and most important being in the world. Soon after he began complimenting her smile, Randy Jr. noticed that Raine took the time to apply makeup and style her hair every day.

She was becoming the sexy woman that he told her she could be. Ordinarily, he wouldn't have looked twice at a woman like Raine. She was homely looking and shy, but he needed her at the moment. Raine was his queen while he was locked inside the prison.

This was his way inside. It didn't take him long before he and Raine were sharing their most intimate details with each other. Raine told Randy Jr. that she was raised by her grandmother after her father shot and killed her mother during a heated argument one night.

She told Randy Jr. that she still kept in touch with her father, but she didn't tell her family about it because it would destroy them. Raine just wanted to be loved. Even though her grandmother raised her and loved her, she wasn't her mother.

Everyone treated Raine like she was a demon seed since she resembled her father. It didn't help that her mother was a petite blond woman and her father was a black man. She faced a great deal of emotional abuse at the hands of her family.

They didn't understand anything about Raine. Her hair, her skin, her body were all completely different from theirs; therefore it was considered ugly. Raine spent her entire life believing that she was ugly.

That was until she met, Randy Jr.

By his third month in prison, Raine gave him a toe curling blowjob inside the storage area of the prison. She shocked Randy Jr. when she told him that she knew exactly where the security cameras were located and offered to help him, "release some tension." At first, he thought she was joking with him.

They fucked in the laundry area while the dryer machines hummed a rhythmic tune. Randy Jr. pounded Raine from behind as she rested her leg on the washing machine. Randy Jr. had more sex inside the prison than he did outside. If it weren't for the tight living quarters, it wouldn't have been so bad. Raine made things that much better.

She loved Randy Jr. so much that she made sure his commissary was full and he received extra privileges. He was working on a way of getting his own prison cell. He needed the privacy to plan his way out of the prison, and he was confident that Raine would be his best asset.

Chapter 10

Sidney sat on the edge of her bed and ran her fingers through her curls. She was finally safe inside her mother's home, away from the questioning eyes of Mystic.

It took a lot of self-control to keep her cool after Randy Jr.'s admission. He kept trying to explain to her that she didn't understand the entire situation. "It's much more complicated than you think, Sidney. Just know that I would never lie to you," he said.

Their drive back home was a long and arduous one. Neither Sidney nor Mystic spoke for nearly an hour of that eight-hour drive. They chose to communicate through music instead, alternating between love ballads with singers belting their apologies to the tunes that belted out angry lyrics with deep resounding bass.

Sidney wanted Mystic to explain what happened that night, but she was afraid that what he would tell her might destroy her.

Her mind reflected on all of the negative things she had been through since she gave her heart to Mystic. His deranged wife tried to kill her. Sidney still couldn't get over that fact. She wanted to ask Mystic what happened to Vondra, but even Sidney didn't want to speak her name.

She had a message on her phone from Vondra's doctor, but Sidney already predicted what the message would say. Even though they were both medical professionals, they couldn't share information about Vondra without her consent. HIPPA laws were stringent, and Sidney understood that no one wanted to be sued. She just wanted to be able to piece together the puzzle that was Vondra Mystic.

Sidney made a note to contact Vondra's Psychiatrist again. When Sidney initially approached Vondra's doctor, she was heading into the FBI Academy. Now that she had graduated and achieved the coveted, Profiler position, things were a bit different. As an FBI Profiler, Sidney could obtain medical records without the constraints of HIPPA regulations.

After considering the situation that she was currently facing, Sidney wondered if Vondra was genuinely crazy or if her husband pushed her in that direction. Sometimes men had a way of driving their woman to the point of losing their minds only to claim that she's too crazy for him. Sidney witnessed it with her friends. Her friend Tynese was still battling with relationship issues that drove her to the point of insanity, so she knew that it was possible.

Sidney didn't know what she expected to hear from Mystic. He was the Chief of Police. Did she really expect the Chief of Police to confess to a crime? What if he admitted to the crime? Sidney mulled over the possibility that her brother could have been mistaken when he saw Mystic, but it just didn't seem likely.

After years of being haunted by the memories from that night, Sidney tried to forget as much as she could, but tried to recall the faces from that night. None of the faces in her mind from that night resembled Mystic's.

The look on Randy Jr.'s face was one of pure anger. After the murder of their father, Randy Jr. often commented that he wanted to learn how to shoot so he could get the men who killed our father.

Sidney resolved to attack her father's killers in a different, more legal manner. When she tried to explain her position to Randy Jr., he called her soft. He told her that she didn't love their daddy if she wanted to be a cop. Sidney would never admit to it, but she was devastated by her brother's words.

Randy Jr. held every Police Officer responsible for the murder of his father, including Sidney if she chose to become one.

If she didn't get to the bottom of the situation soon, she was sure that Randy Jr. would, and she didn't have time for that chaos.

She wiped her tears and cried softly as she recalled his words. "Sidney, I was a young rookie cop. I had no control over anything," he pleaded finally after she gave him the silent treatment for nearly the entire ride back home. She was relieved when his resolve finally broke, and he turned to face her and ceased the silence with his words.

"Sidney, you have to believe me. I have no idea what your brother was talking about," Mystic explained with a look of sadness. "I would never lie to you. I love you," he said as he held her hand gently.

His reaction only piqued Sidney's interests as her reminiscing ceased.

The bright sunshine peaking in her window, welcomed Sidney back to Miami, but something deep inside told Sidney that things would forever be changed. Sidney was still intrigued by what her brother Randy Jr. told her about the man that makes her heart beat fast. She retrieved the file that Garcia gave her and poured herself a glass of wine.

As she read the Police Report dated July 8, 1992, Sidney's eyes widened with shock. According to the report, an emergency call came in at 3:08 am from a concerned neighbor.

The neighbor reported a domestic disturbance at the Stevens residence next door. Five officers responded to the call that night, and after witnessing Randy Stevens Sr. physically assaulting his wife, they arrested him for battery. According to the report, Randy Stevens Sr. resisted arrest.

The further she read, the more upset she grew. Sidney began to remember that night, well. She could still hear her father yelling at the cops and her mother begging them to let him go. She remembered the look on Randy Sr.'s face as the three cops carried him out of the house. Sidney took a break from the file and began to cry uncontrollably.

Florence heard the sobs and quickly ran to her room. She asked Sidney, "What happened, are you, okay sweetheart?"

Sidney's beautiful caramel face was beet red and wet with tears. "I'm ok mom, just thinking about old times when daddy was here, the funny jokes he used to tell and the kisses on my forehead he used to give me. I know that I'm being silly right now!"

Florence's concerned expression softened as she sat down next to her daughter. "No sweetheart, you're not. I try to have my breakdowns while you are at work and Cero is asleep. I miss him too Sid, 32 years of being with one person wasn't easy but I just can't and won't accept that he is gone. My husband is gone."

Florence and Sidney held each other until their tears subsided. Florence wiped her tears and cleared her throat. "Looks like you're busy. Just remember to take a break, Sidney. If not you'll burn yourself out," she advised as she kissed her daughter's forehead and left the room.

Sidney wiped her eyes with the back of her hand and took a deep breath. She had to keep it together if she wanted to get to the bottom of everything.

Sidney's eyes scanned the document, searching for the names that were listed under, "Responding Officers" and her eyes widened with surprise. Although she shouldn't have been surprised by the fact that the report withheld critical information. The only information that she was searching for was missing from the document.

Badge numbers were listed in place of the Officer's names. Sidney rolled her eyes in frustration. The Department would do anything to protect their own. She knew that the names were omitted to protect the responding officers. Sidney couldn't wait to expose all of them and their corruption.

She squinted and read the numbers carefully.

Strangely enough, all of the badge numbers were handwritten in blue ink. Sidney wondered why someone would scribble across an official document. She noted the badge numbers, with the goal in mind to research each Police Officer there that night.

She remembered her patient Sly who was in love with Norman. Sidney still thought about Sly and his obsession with Norman. She would never forget Norman's face. Sidney wondered what his badge number was. Now that she had the document in her hand, Sidney was on an investigative mission.

She had a plan to find out who her father's killers were and she was well on her way there. She considered who could help her get the rest of her plan off without a hitch and only one name came to mind.

Sidney questioned herself, wondering if she could ever trust Mystic. Then she recalled the hand that they located in her brother's safe. Mystic managed to stay quiet about what they found, for now. She wondered how much longer he would remain quiet.

She figured that would be his biggest test. She would test Mystic's integrity and loyalty to her by his ability to keep her brother's suspected additional crimes a secret.

Sidney had to tread carefully with regards to Mystic, because of what he knew. She couldn't afford for Randy Jr. to have additional time added to his sentence.

Sidney considered her next option, then picked up her phone. When the phone rang for the fifth time she was about to give up on her plan. Suddenly, the voicemail greeting began to play as Sidney considered whether she should leave a message.

Throwing caution to the wind, Sidney began to speak after the beep. "Hi, Dr. Streeter this is Sidney Stevens. When you have the opportunity, please call me," she said as she rattled off the phone number on the message.

Sidney prayed that her former professor at the FBI Academy could come through for her because at the moment she didn't trust anyone.

Chapter 11

Marcus Mystic appraised his reflection in the mirror with a smile. His bright green eyes sparkled with charm and charisma. His skin was the color of café au lait, and his smile could make any woman melt. For years he got by on his looks and his charm. He did climb through the ranks of the Police Department rather quickly, based on his experience and knowledge which he so prominently displayed, daily.

He thought about Sidney every minute of the day when he was apart from her. It bothered Mystic that he couldn't get through to Sidney. He loved her desperately, but he also knew that he couldn't say but so much. Although he cared about Sidney, he also cared about his job and his lifestyle that he worked so hard for.

Mystic hated keeping secrets, and he despised scandal. Currently, he was involved in a huge scandal. He still had Killa Dre's hand in his possession. He knew that the heat would come down on him hard if someone found out that he knew who was behind the slaying of Killa Dre.

Killa Dre's death was a great benefit to the community because the drugs he sold and controlled in the neighborhood was to their detriment. Mystic knew that Killa

Dre's murder wouldn't wholly eliminate drug abuse in the community, but it would slow it down considerably until a new gangster took over.

Mystic didn't miss Killa Dre, but he knew that someone would. He knew personally that a few officers were on Killa Dre's payroll. He surmised that they would try to investigate the death of Killa Dre to avenge him.

Killa Dre's criminal empire kept food on the table for some of the most unlikely individuals. It unnerved Mystic that he had to actually cover for Randy Jr., but Mystic couldn't think of another way to fix the situation with the love of his life and winning her trust back.

Mystic couldn't win.

Sidney was pissed with him, and he didn't know how to get her to believe in him again. Mystic considered that if he turned in Killa Dre's hand and affirmed where he located the hand, Randy Jr. wouldn't stand a chance. He would never be let out of prison with an additional murder charge on his record.

Mystic considered the idea. Randy Jr. hated him. He knew a few things that Sidney didn't. Mystic wondered if he let Randy Jr. rot in prison how long it would take before Sidney forgot about the accusations he hurled at Mystic during the prison visitation. He wondered if he would ever get Sidney back in his arms.

That was only one of his troubles.

Vondra was posed to cause him some serious issues if she didn't calm down in the mental hospital. He estimated locking her away at the North Florida Mental

Hospital was a great temporary solution to his troubles, but he could tell that something wasn't working correctly. Vondra called him daily, nonstop.

Vera called him just as often as Vondra. Mystic ignored her incessant calls. He blocked the hospital number from his cell phone and told himself that he would deal with it when he was ready. Mystic couldn't tell his aunt about the issue because he really didn't want to speak with anyone at the hospital. So, he ignored every call that came through his phone, unless it came from his office.

Mystic wanted to just bury Vondra at the hospital and walk away, forever. He begged his aunt for help, and Vera quickly jumped into action. He considered contacting Vera to tell her that Vondra had somehow obtained telephone privileges. That way he could stop the incessant phone calls. She left him messages, over 100 per day. Mystic simply deleted the messages he received from the hospital.

He no longer cared.

Now that he was the Chief of Police he had real things to worry about. He didn't have time to chase behind his wife to make sure that she was taking her medication and abiding by the law. It was too tiring for Mystic.

The two women in his life were both driving him crazy.

Chapter 12

"What's going on?" Spencer asked as his eyes scanned the room, searching for the Police. "Where are the cops?" he asked as Artie chuckled loudly.

"Sweetheart, what are you talking about?" he asked as Spencer rubbed his forehead, confused. It took him a minute to realize that he was safe in Artie's house and not in a prison cell. He was losing his mind.

"Oh, thank goodness. It was only a dream," Spencer sighed with relief.

Artie shot Spencer an apprehensive glance. "Spencer, are you feeling ok?" he asked as Spencer nodded his head and sat up on the couch.

"Man, you have been sleeping for hours. I didn't want to disturb you. I know for a fact that you didn't sleep last night," Artie explained. Spencer knew what Artie was referring too, the box. Spencer didn't know what to do when the box was delivered to Artie's front doorstep. Artie opened the box and dropped it on the floor. Spencer watched as a seasoned Police Officer grabbed his stomach and vomited at the sight.

Against his better judgment, Spencer took a look inside the box and screamed at the sight of Linda's mouth. He knew exactly who the culprit was; it was Steven. He knew that Steven would be back to finish his job. He was only trying to scare Spencer for the fun of it.

Spencer had no doubt that Steven was watching his every move.

How else would he have known that Spencer was at Artie's house that night? Spencer considered his dream just before Artie woke him up. In his dream, he was arrested for Linda's murder. Spencer wondered if it was an omen. Did he have something to worry about? Steven was crazy enough to try and frame him for the murder of Linda.

As he considered the thought, a shudder ran up his spine. Spencer really wasn't sure if he didn't kill Linda that night. He tried to forget about the details of that evening, but he wasn't confident that he didn't contribute to Linda's death.

Just the thought of Linda made his erection grow. Linda was one of a kind. She elicited feelings from Spencer that he never felt before. Linda was the only woman who made him orgasm and not just any orgasm, she made his entire body shake and tremble with satisfaction. Spencer would never forget his experience with Linda.

At night he was haunted with visions of himself stabbing Linda. Spencer hoped that it wasn't true. He couldn't fathom being considered a murderer. He didn't have it in him. Spencer wasn't the thug type of guy; he was more of a lover than a fighter.

His bronze complexion and physically fit body, coupled with penetrating hazel eyes were too titillating to waste on violence.

He couldn't imagine himself harming anyone, but every time he envisioned himself shuddering with an orgasm he saw his hands tight around Linda's throat. She made his body feel so good. Linda used her kegel muscles to pull Spencer's hardness in and push him out at will.

Her wetness was too much for him to handle. It was maddening. Linda climbed on top of Spencer and spun around on him like she was a gymnast. Spencer never experienced anything like it before. He and Linda shared a toe-curling orgasm and collapsed in the bed.

He remembered feeling ashamed after he had an orgasm.

Spencer had visions of choking Linda. His manhood was shoved deep in her throat as she professionally and skillfully coaxed his erection. Linda prepared him for Steven. Spencer remembered having the time of his life that night with Linda and Steven. The sounds of lovemaking went well into the night as they pleased and tasted each other.

Sex was always a release for Spencer, but he feared that this time he got much more than he could have ever bargained for. His night of pleasure with Linda and Steven could cost him his life.

The mere thought of it made Spencer's voice catch in his throat when he heard his name called again. "Yes?" he answered as Garcia walked towards him and repeated his question. "I said, are you alright? I have to go for my run," Garcia mentioned while he waited for Spencer to respond.

Spencer looked up from the couch and noticed that Artie was fully dressed and ready to go for a run. He was wearing electric blue running shorts and a blue and green tank top. Spencer licked his lips as his eyes roamed over Artie's muscular body. He noticed the sweat glistening on Artie's massive arms.

Spencer didn't respond to Artie.

He dropped to the floor and crawled towards Artie. When he looked up at Artie, Spencer was still on his knees licking his lips with anticipation. Artie smiled seductively at Spencer. He knew what Spencer was up to and he wasn't about to stop him. He noticed Spencer's massive erection poking through his shorts and considered canceling his run.

Spencer took Artie deep in his mouth as Artie leaned back and moaned loudly. "Ooh yeah. Show me how much you love it," Artie said as he watched Spencer take him in and out of his mouth in a manner so seductive it was artistic. Artie started speaking in Spanish as Spencer continued with his skillful blowjob.

Spencer couldn't understand what Artie was saying, and he didn't respond, verbally that is.

Chapter 13

Officer Arturo Garcia ran along the Miami shoreline pumping his fists and legs, his feet pounded the pavement as he sprinted. The sun was shining, and it was over 80 degrees outside, it was indeed a perfect day for a run.

The breeze that came off the Atlantic Ocean was intoxicating. In his opinion, there was no better place to live than sunny Miami, Florida.

Although his body was present in Miami, his mind was far away from there.

His mind was on Spencer. His sun-kissed skin, the way he smiled when he was being playful and even his deep throat were all the things that made Spencer Artie's soul mate. He couldn't imagine his life without Spencer.

No other man or woman made him feel so content and at peace like Spencer. Garcia's mind kept flashing back to the day he received the box. He wished that there was something that he could do to help his friend. As he ran, he racked his brain trying to find a way to help Spencer out of the situation.

He had to do something with the package he received. Arturo was a veteran Police Officer, and he was also aware that what he was doing would be considered a crime. He had to find a way to get rid of the evidence that was delivered to his doorstep without bringing any heat on himself.

Garcia didn't want to lose his hard-earned status or his salary. He depended on his salary to live as well as he felt he deserved. Garcia didn't want to see it all end over the situation that Spencer brought to his doorstep. He had to stay focused on the real reason he was there.

Sex was spectacular, but it wasn't enough to keep him sustained for his life. He needed his job to provide and pay the bills. Although he tried to push the thought from his mind, he couldn't help but think that Spencer was becoming a liability in his life.

He wanted to get Spencer out of his system, but it wasn't an easy thing. Spencer made him feel so good it was invigorating. Being within Spencer's company felt like standing in the middle of the spotlight. Spencer made Garcia feel like a real man.

Although he firmly believed that his family would eventually be supportive, Garcia never came out of the closet as a gay man. He knew that it would take them a long time to adjust to his lifestyle, but they would decide, ultimately that he meant more than any judgment.

That's what he wanted to believe, but Garcia knew that it would be completely different once he actually came out. His mother and sister were the only real family that he had, and they depended on him.

They looked up to him as the Garcia who had it all together. It made him sad when he thought about the false hopes his family had about him. They thought that he was perfect.

They had no idea that he had a secret life. Both his mother and sister are devout Christians. His mother, Rosa Garcia would collapse from the shock of her son being a sinner.

Her son, the saint, her son who was in a state of confusion in his own mind. He still had his sights set on Sidney.

Chapter 14

Vondra sipped on ice-cold water as she headed towards her sister's house. Based on the address that she stole, she would be at her sister's home in an hour. Vondra didn't care how long it took; she was determined to reach her destination. She had to get to her son, and then her plan would begin.

It took some work to get ahold of Elsa's home address. Lawrence was a valuable asset. Vondra laughed hysterically as she recalled the look on Lawrence's face when she shoved the needle into his veins.

Lawrence was an orderly at the North Florida Mental Hospital, but he wielded his power over everyone in the hospital. Vondra nearly gagged as she recalled the favors that she had to give Lawrence in order to gain access to certain amenities.

Although he made her skin crawl, Vondra enjoyed giving Lawrence sexual favors. He was a chubby, greasy looking guy, so Vondra didn't estimate that he had a harem of women. Instead, she pegged Lawrence as a virgin when she first laid eyes on him. She let Lawrence assume that he had full control over her. One evening when he entered her room, she was fully naked and waiting for him.

"I have something for you," she offered as she raised her leg higher to show a perfectly plucked vagina. Lawrence jumped back with surprise, but she could tell by the look on his face that he was pleased. Vondra took it as a sign to continue with her behavior. She took her index finger and sucked on it slowly, eyeing Lawrence as he rubbed the growing bulge in the front of his pants.

When Vondra inserted her index finger inside her vagina, Lawrence quivered with pleasure. Vondra removed her index finger and used it to summon Lawrence to the bed. Lawrence turned the lock on her door and flipped the light switch off as he moved slowly towards Vondra in the darkness.

The minute Vondra felt his hot breath in her ear, she knew that she had Lawrence wrapped around her finger. She pushed Lawrence on the bed and straddled him. Lawrence quivered with excitement and pleasure when she thrust him inside of her and arched her back.

Vondra moved her hips and body rhythmically as Lawrence moaned and groaned with pleasure. She could tell by his rhythm that he was inexperienced and that made her more excited. Vondra took pleasure in making Lawrence whine and cry out in passion. After that first night, Vondra had Lawrence right where she needed him.

Although she never put it on him like she did the first time, Lawrence kept coming back for more. He was sure to check in on Vondra every evening when the lights went out. Her final night with Lawrence was just as routine as before. Vondra waited until Lawrence entered her room late that evening. She beckoned him inside her room and straddled him. Vondra made Lawrence beg to be inserted inside of her.

When she finally obliged his body trembled and jerked in an orgasmic seizure that made Vondra even more excited. Vondra straddled Lawrence and writhed on top of him until he shouted out, "Mercy!" Then she sprung into action, inserting the syringe in his neck to administer the deadly concoction into his bloodstream.

She only had a few minutes to access the computer, locate Elsa's address and escape.

Vondra had been planning her escape since her first day inside the facility. She knew that if they conducted additional mental health assessments, she would be stuck in the hospital forever. She wondered what was taking Mystic so long to visit her.

Everything seemed so strange to Vondra. She knew who was behind her husband's sudden change, that bitch Sidney. Vondra made a plan to attack Sidney the minute she had her son with her. She would take Sidney out and then she would introduce Mystic to their son. They would be a family again. By the time he thought about Sidney, she would be food for the worms.

Vondra laughed hysterically at the thought.

The further she drove the more Vondra considered what she would do to her sister once she arrived. Vondra stared at the address as tears filled her eyes, "why would she go back there?"

Vondra expected Elsa to be surprised when she showed up to retrieve her son because Elsa would never expect Vondra to show up there...NEVER!

Chapter 15

Spencer stood in the middle of the swim center floor trying his best to regain his composure. He had just received another package in the mail. It was a still image with Spencer standing behind Linda, pleasuring her doggy style.

Spencer stared at the picture. He wanted to shred it like the rest, but he couldn't stop staring at the look of passion on his face.

Every week like clockwork, Spencer received a letter in the mail containing an image. He knew who was behind it all. Steven was deranged. He wrote poems about missing Spencer. He wrote about how much he loved Spencer.

Spencer couldn't believe any of his lies.

He didn't trust Steven.

It broke his heart to think about his time with Linda. The longer he stared at the picture, the more he realized how much he cared for Linda.

Although she wasn't the most beautiful woman, Linda had a sweet spirit and a heart of gold. Spencer couldn't imagine how much better Linda's life would have turned out if she never met Steven.

He thought about his dream at Artie's house. Spencer hoped that everything would be alright with Linda's case, but something told him that he was mistaken.

Snapping his fingers with the realization of why he was in the swim area Spencer walked to the back of the swim area. He found his locker in the bank of cabinets and typed in the code. Once the lock opened, Spencer retrieved a Balenciaga shoe box.

Inside the shoebox, he placed the picture. The box was already filled with notes and pictures from Steven. Spencer didn't know what to do with the junk that Steven sent to him, but he figured he could use it in a harassment lawsuit against Steven later.

Once Spencer opened the lid on the box, the first image he saw was of Linda's mouth, full with Spencer's long thick member. Spencer was shaken by the picture. He wanted to make the entire night with Linda disappear, but he knew in his heart that his night with Linda would be forever etched in his mind.

It was the last time everything made sense.

"Spencer, please come to the front you have a visitor," a voice reported over the microphone system. Sighing with frustration, Spencer turned and headed towards the front of the building. He loved his job, and it was a welcomed distraction.

"Act normal," Artie advised Spencer. "Go to work, take care of your business. Don't give anyone any idea of your involvement in that stuff," Artie advised to Spencer's delight. Spencer was grateful that he had Artie Garcia in his back pocket, or so he thought.

He knew that sleeping with cops would one day pay off. As he walked back to the office, images of his time with Artie earlier that morning flashed before his eyes. Spencer inhaled deeply with a smile on his face. He could still smell Artie's cologne on him.

Spencer refused to take a shower that morning, He rushed into work smelling like Artie. It didn't matter to him. He wanted to have the reminder that he had someone with him in all of this.

He wasn't funky of course. He did the usual wipe off, but he was sure not to wipe anywhere near his neck. That was Artie's favorite place on him.

Spencer wondered who would be visiting him in the gym. It had been a few days since he worked, so his schedule was pretty clear. When he reached the front, he nearly passed out.

A handsome brown-skinned Police Officer was standing in the front wearing a knowing grin. Ordinarily, Spencer would have been excited, but the Officer didn't look as if he was there for fitness help.

Spencer took in a deep breath and willed himself to continue walking. Spencer wanted to turn around and run. Once he reached the Officer, he extended his right hand to Spencer. "Hi Spencer McIntyre?" he asked as Spencer nodded slowly. "Hey buddy, I'm Detective Kyle Long. I have a few questions to ask you. Do you have somewhere private where we can talk for a few minutes?" Detective Long asked looking around the gym.

Chapter 16

Sidney stood in front of the long mirror hanging in the hallway, outside her bedroom. She was preparing for her first day in the office since the FBI Academy graduation. Sidney couldn't wait to start her new job. She loved her previous job as a therapist, but this new position promised to be a challenge. Sidney welcomed the new challenge of her status as an FBI Profiler. She desperately needed something to take her mind off her current situation.

Mystic had been calling her and texting her, daily. He left brief messages, merely apologizing for putting her through all of this. She didn't understand why he wouldn't just come clean and explain to her what happened that night.

She knew that he was there. She read the notarized report that stated as much. It just frustrated Sidney that he would rather apologize profusely but do nothing to remedy what he did wrong.

"You on your way to work, Sid?" her mother called out from her bedroom. Florence was in her room still in bed. Sidney had never seen anything like it before.

Her mother never lounged in the bed, and if she did oversleep, Florence was always awake before Sidney. She walked inside her mother's bedroom and flipped the switch on the lamp near Florence's bed.

"Momma, are you feeling alright?" Sidney asked as she placed a loving hand on her mother's forehead to check her temperature. Florence chuckled but ended up in a coughing fit. Sidney sprinted out of the bedroom and headed towards the kitchen. She grabbed some water for her mother and then quickly returned to her bedside.

Florence slowly drank the water under Sidney's watchful eye. "Momma is everything alright?" Sidney questioned as she surveyed her mother for any signs of distress.

Florence smiled and pat her daughter's shoulder lovingly. "I'm fine, baby," she said between coughs and slow sips of water. "I just don't know what's come over me. I feel worn out," she explained as Sidney nodded.

"Momma, I can stay here and help you with Cero," Sidney offered as she stared lovingly at her mother. Florence Stevens was indeed a diamond in the rough. She had experienced so much turmoil and strife in her life; it made Sidney sad that she couldn't do more for her mother.

Her mother was a rare, precious flower that didn't bloom properly in the ghetto. It bothered Sidney that she couldn't move her family out of their current situation.

She considered her new full-time position and smiled to herself. She would make sure that she moved her mother and brother out of the hell hole before it killed them all.

Florence laid back down on the pillow and closed her eyes. "Honey, fix Cero a sandwich before you leave. I'll be up in a bit," she said slowly as Sidney watched her mother with tears in her eyes.

"Mom, if you're not better when I get back, I'm taking you to the hospital," Sidney assured as her mother nodded in agreement, already half-asleep. She looked so small curled up in her queen-sized bed. She kept the house in the same manner that it was when her husband lived in it.

Sidney felt a pang of sadness for her mother when she glanced at their wedding picture hanging up over their bed. Poor Florence loved her husband, dearly. She didn't date or talk about dating other men. Florence believed that as long as she was alive, she would be Mrs. Randy Stevens Sr.

It saddened Sidney how much her mother loved her father. She couldn't imagine loving a man for over thirty years, knowing that he couldn't ever return to her.

Sidney opened her brother Cero's door and peeked inside. He was still curled up in his bed. Cero was a teenager, but he still had stuffed animals lining his bedroom walls to keep him company. Sidney treated her brother as a baby.

He made Sidney proud, but he also wore out their family. Sidney planted a kiss on his forehead, which he quickly wiped away. "Good morning, Cero," she sang as he smiled then his eyes fluttered open.

Sidney loved her brother's sweet innocence. "Morning, Sid," he said kissing her cheek. "Are you hungry?" she asked as he shook his head vigorously telling her that he was not interested in eating anything.

"Well, I'm going to make you a PB&J sandwich," Sidney offered as Cero clapped his hands with excitement. "PBJ!" he shouted as she laughed. "Cero, Momma isn't feeling well today. Can you help take care of her?" Sidney asked as she watched her brother consider her question.

"Momma sick?" he asked as he flapped his hands in frustration. "No, no Cero. She's ok. She just needs rest. Can you let her rest today?" Sidney asked as she tried to calm her brother back down.

"Help? Rest" he said as she nodded in agreement. "Yes, help rest," he said as he laid back down on the bed and pretended to be asleep. Sidney laughed at her brother and headed towards the kitchen.

To her surprise, Florence was standing in front of the stove frying bacon. "Momma, I thought you were tired?" Sidney asked. "I can do it," she said taking the spatula from her mother. "Please lay back down," Sidney pleaded.

"No, honey. I have to send Cero to school early this morning. They have a field trip today. He's excited about going," Florence added with a smile. "I will rest once he gets on the bus. I promise," she said knowing full well that she wouldn't rest any longer.

Sidney kissed her mother's cheek again and promised that she would call her to check on her later that day.

Sidney knew that she had a full caseload so her day would be especially busy, but she didn't care.

She loved helping people heal.

As soon as she reached the outside air, she hit "Send" on her phone and listened as it dialed her brother's attorney. She was so anxious to hear from him that she was nearly hyperventilating when he answered the phone.

"Mr. Billingsley please tell me that you have some good news for me?" Sidney pleaded as she heard Mr. Billingsley take in a deep breath. "I'm not going to sugar coat it, your brother is facing some serious charges, Sidney," he said with certainty.

"Your brother asked that I continue to send you money to help provide for you and your mother," he stated. Sidney considered his words for a moment then finally asked, "What kind of money?" she recalled the money inside her brother's safe, but didn't quite know if that was enough to provide for the long term.

"Your brother has established a fund with you as the executor. I will be in touch with you soon. Maybe we can schedule a time to meet?" he asked hopefully. Sidney rolled her eyes in the air. She knew what Mr. Billingsley was trying to do.

"Sure, please make sure that you stay on top of my brother's case," she begged as he assured her that he had Randy Jr. at the top of his priority list.

When Sidney returned from Atlanta, she told her mother that Randy Jr. was staying with a girlfriend in

Tallahassee. She said that he would call her once he got enough money to add minutes to his phone.

Florence didn't know any better and as long as Sidney didn't seem frightened she was fine with Randy Jr.'s excuse. "I just wish he'd call me," she said in response to her daughter's explanation.

Sidney asked Mr. Billingsley to have her brother call home. It was about time that he came clean to his mother and told her the truth. Especially since he faced a possible life sentence.

Chapter 17

Lucy typed the beginning of the legal brief with her mind nowhere near the Law Firm. Since the minute she laid eyes on her grandson behind bars, her mind had been inside the prison with him. Lucy was working with Raoul's Public Defender,

She wanted to get Raoul out of that madhouse with the hardened criminals. This was his first chargeable offense, after all. Lucy was adamant that her grandson is released. Her baby was just a misunderstood child. He didn't belong in there with killers and rapists, but it wasn't looking good.

Raoul had become hardened, acting out. Following in the footsteps of Tulea. He had been involved in several fights and had been moved to solitary confinement. He was dealt a hand that he can't place on the table being that his mother was addicted to heroin and his father was a felon serving a life sentence.

Lucy just knew in her heart and prayed that once the jury heard the details of Raoul's tragic life, they would spare him, but his actions inside of prison displayed his truth.

She was heartbroken to find that they were willing to send her baby to prison for 36 months. Lucy wailed when they announced the verdict. Her grandson showed no emotion, his face was bruised, and his front tooth was missing.

His grandmother cried out to God for help. Lucy couldn't imagine her baby in that place for 36 months. She knew deep within her soul, he would probably never make it out. She barely recognized him when she saw him. Little did she know, that would be her last time seeing him.

Her innocent Raoul fought for his life, but in the end, he paid for the sins of his father, unbeknownst to him. Tulea sold him out.

Lucy knew that Tulea would get his hands on her baby if he remained confined within the walls of the prison. Lucy was determined to get Raoul away from Tulea and away from prison. She already felt the loss of one child to Tulea, now the news of her grandson was too much to bear.

She was convinced that Tulea got her daughter, Halle hooked on drugs. He was most definitely to blame for her abandonment of their only child. Halle lost complete control of her mind when the US Marshals kicked in Lucy's door, searching for Tulea.

She watched her daughter stand in between Tulea and the cop's gun. It destroyed Lucy to witness her daughter willing to die for this trash of a man when she had a child in the room, an infant depending upon her.

It was that moment where Lucy realized that she failed as a mother. Her daughter had no compassion for the pure. She cared nothing about the innocent. Halle only cared about one person, Tulea.

Lucy tried to shake the past from her mind as she sat on the couch with Raoul's picture in her hand. Tears streamed down her face as she ended the call with the Medical Examiner's office requesting her to come down to identify the remains of her grandson and to pick up his personal effects. The one person she was responsible for, her heartbeat, her little man, her only grandson was gone.

Lucy was numb. She looked in her purse to find the cell number that Sidney gave her before she left, and she called, but it went straight to voicemail. Lucy laid her head back against the couch and screamed out asking God why? She had no way of contacting her daughter to let her know what happened. Lucy felt defeated, she felt as if she had once again failed and just couldn't stop sobbing.

She dried her face and talked herself into getting it together and doing what she knew had to be done.

Lucy arrived at the ME's office and was directed to the appropriate room to make the proper identification of her grandson.

Lucy had to be helped to a chair as she saw Raoul lying there with knife wounds all over his small body. She then noticed the letter "T" carved on his stomach which solidified in her mind that Tulea caused his death. This was her fear, her nightmare was a reality. Lucy felt that she had nothing else to live for.

After signing all of the paperwork for the Medical Examiner, Lucy knew what she had to do next, being in the frame of mind that she was in, she drove herself to the Behavioral Health Hospital. Her voices were overpowering her, and her

thoughts of wanting to go with Raoul were strong.

"Hi, my name is Lucy Davis, and I need to check myself in. I don't want to live anymore." The attendant nodded at Lucy and responded. "Right this way Ms. Davis, it's been a while!"

Chapter 18

She busied herself in the kitchen as she waited patiently for her daughter to leave the apartment. Florence loved having Sidney at home with her. She always knew how to take excellent care of her.

It had been over three decades for Florence with one man in her life, the love of her life. All she cared about was her dear deceased husband, but loneliness began to creep in when her children were away.

Earl Davenport was Florence's good friend. They met decades ago when Earl moved with his young family to the projects. Their family was originally from Maryland. Earl moved them all down to Florida for a brand new start.

He had no idea what he was getting into when they moved into the projects, but Earl worked hard to keep his family together.

Earl and Eva, his wife, worked two jobs each. That's where Florence came in. She watched over their children late at night. She kept them comfortable inside her loving home while both of them worked. It made Florence feel useful to have children to depend on her, and she needed the extra cash.

Cero enjoyed playing with their two young boys. They played Super Mario Brothers together and treated Cero well. She never had to speak to them about teasing her son. That made her feel great.

It was sad to see Earl's wife, Eva deteriorate before her eyes. She died from brain cancer within three months of her diagnosis. Her death broke Earl all the way down, especially since they had just sent their youngest child to college. Earl was broken inside.

No one understood, but Florence.

She felt like she owed Earl some compassion. He was the only person who offered her kindness when she needed it most.

If it weren't for Earl, Florence wouldn't have been able to purchase many of the Christmas gifts that she bought for her children when she and Randy Sr. fell short. She would never let her husband know that her friend was helping her make their holidays happy.

Sadly that same year, besides Earl losing his wife to cancer, he lost his daughter in a tragic car accident.

Heartbroken and alone, Earl turned to Florence for prayer and guidance. Florence introduced him to her grief support group, Healing Hands. The group met twice weekly, and they helped each other cope with losing loved ones, tragically.

Florence felt like she had to help Earl when she watched how lonely he looked without his wife, Eva. She finally worked up enough nerve to invite him to a

Healing Hands meeting. When Earl began attending the meetings, Florence was thrilled to see the change in him.

The two were becoming close and shared more in common than they cared to acknowledge because of their lost loved ones.

Florence felt terrible about keeping her new friendship from her kids a secret. She hated keeping secrets from them. For years she begged them to be honest and open with her, and here she was holding this back from them but she didn't want to give them the wrong idea.

The one thing that was of certainty here is that Florence needed Earls friendship just as much as Earl needed hers. After getting Cero on the school bus, Florence returned to the house, meeting Earl on the porch, invited him in and poured two cups of coffee, and sliced two pieces of her fresh coffee cake for them both as they sat down in the kitchen and chatted the morning away.

Chapter 19

Spencer escorted the handsome Police Detective to his office in the back and pointed to the chairs. "Please have a seat," he offered coyly.

"Mr. McIntyre, I am investigating the murder of Linda King. I was wondering if you knew of the victim," he asked as Spencer nodded. "Yes, Linda and her husband Steven were clients of mine," Spencer added without elaborating.

The Detective took note of his hesitation and responded. "I see," he said as he continued with his barrage of questions. "When was the last time you saw Linda King?" he asked as Spencer shrugged his shoulders.

"She had a fitness session in the gym several days ago," Spencer added with a nonchalant wave. The Detective's eyebrows arched inquisitively as he questioned Spencer's time frame, "Are you sure that was the last time you saw her?" he asked.

Spencer looked down at the floor then out the window before he responded. He knew that the moment he answered the question, he would become Public Enemy #1.

The Detective sighed loudly as he waited for Spencer's response. The responding Detective seemed to be a seasoned professional. He had the power of discernment. He appeared as if he could look at someone and tell if they were evasive.

Spencer was evasive.

The Detective quietly watched Spencer as he tried to explain his way out of whatever he was trying to hide. He already knew that Spencer was lying, but he continued to ask pointed questions to see how much longer he would wiggle and squirm.

"Do you remember what time that was?" he inquired as he opened his blank notepad. He carried around his notebook to keep his notes handy and also to intimidate possible perpetrators into spilling the beans.

When a perpetrator witnessed him jotting down what they said, they grew nervous; especially when they were telling a lie. "Uhh..maybe at 3pm," Spencer responded as the officer continued questioning Spencer.

Spencer dodged some of the questions, but he found himself in a pickle when the Detective began repeating his answers back to him for confirmation.

Finally, the Detective sighed loudly and placed his notebook on the table beside Spencer. "Spencer, can I level with you for a minute?" he asked as Spencer nodded.

"I know that you and Linda had a love affair. I know that you saw Linda outside of this place," he said opening his arms wide in a demonstration. "I know more than you think I know, Spencer. So it would be in your best interests if you simply told the truth," he said watching Spencer closely.

Spencer squirmed in the seat and rested his head in his hands for a moment while he thought about the predicament that he was in. "Sir, you have to understand that I didn't do anything wrong," Spencer pleaded as the Police Detective listened to him without showing any facial expression.

"I spent the night with Linda and Steven," Spencer confessed as the Detective leaned forward in his seat, intrigued by Spencer's sudden revelation. "I don't remember much about that night. I know that we had sex," he said as the Detective nodded and continued writing.

"I woke up the next day, and I couldn't remember anything about the night before. I think Steven drugged me," Spencer accused. He watched as the Detective showed no emotion and continued writing.

"When I touched Linda she was ice cold and covered in blood," Spencer cried as the Detective listened to him, eyeing him carefully. He never moved to comfort Spencer.

Spencer wiped at his tears and continued to explain his position to the Detective. "I know that I didn't kill Linda!" he said as the Detective nodded. Spencer continued to explain how he was at the SIZZLE parade partying it up one minute then the next he was in Steven's bed.

He tried to tell the Detective how he was stalked by Steven. Spencer considered showing him his box of still images but then thought against it. He had already said and done way too much without an attorney present.

Spencer prayed silently that he didn't seal his own fate by telling the Detective everything he knew without consulting a lawyer, first. He knew that it was too late to consider a lawyer now. He already placed himself in Linda's house at the time of her death. He told the Detective about their torrid threesome.

It was all out in the open.

Spencer tried to re-explain his situation to the Detective, but he held up a hand to stop him from talking.

"Spencer, I think that it would be in your best interest if you hired an attorney," the Detective added as he began to stand. "As I said, I am investigating the murder of Linda King, and I would hate for you to implicate yourself," he advised.

Chapter 20

Mystic walked inside the vast state of the art building and winked at the security guard seated in front. "Good morning, Chief. How are you doing today?" Rodney, their faithful security guard asked as Mystic grinned at him. "I'm doing well. How are you?" he asked as the gentleman responded. "I can't complain," and opened the door for Mystic to bypass the security counter.

Although he was promoted to Chief of Police, Mystic still carried a secondary weapon on him. It made him feel comfortable. After all the years in the field, Mystic was used to being on patrol. He loved being the Chief of Police because it came with much more money and clout, but he was still a street cop at heart.

Mystic greeted his secretary as he walked inside the glass-walled office. "Good morning, sir," she said with a bright smile. Stephanie Abli was his new secretary.

Long legs and short natural hair, Stephanie was a lovely sight. She was as efficient as she was stunning. When his supervisor introduced him to Stephanie, Mystic smiled widely knowing that he would enjoy every second at work.

His buddy in Human Resources felt the same.

Although he put on a brave face, it was all a front. Mystic couldn't get his mind off of his situation with Sidney. It was all spiraling out of control. Just like his mental state, Mystic was losing control in every area of his life.

He couldn't sleep, he didn't eat anything. All he could do was think about the mistakes he made in his life. Mystic would have given anything to go back to that fateful night. If he could, he would have done so many things differently.

Sidney had to understand how much he loved her. Mystic wished that he never went inside the Police precinct to see Randy Jr. Things would have been so much better. He would have had more control over how Sidney found out about his involvement that night.

Now he had no control over anything. Mystic's stomach lurched uncomfortably as he vomited in the trash can. He was a mess. "I gotta get myself together," he told himself wiping his mouth with a napkin. He felt just as guilty as he did the last night he saw Randy Sr.

He had hoped and prayed that with time his guilt would have lessened, but it didn't.

Mystic carried this guilt with him from that night until now. He even went to the funeral, and sat in the back of the church, and watched Sidney break down as they closed the casket. He slipped out just as quietly as he slipped in.

Witnessing that beautiful young girl suffer from unimaginable heartache shattered Mystic inside. He wanted to help her, to make a difference in her life. Although his reasoning was selfish, he wanted the very best for Sidney. He just wished that he could get her to understand it.

Chapter 21

Randy Jr. watched closely as one of his customers snorted a line of cocaine in front of him. When his customers' eyes widened from the adrenaline, Randy Jr. clapped his hands together and requested payment.

"Alright, that's $45," Randy Jr. announced as the inmate and Randy Jr. exchanged money for drugs quickly. All of this occurred under the watchful eyes of the prison guards. Randy Jr. was quickly amassing a fortune in the prison, and he had one person to thank for it all, his girl Ciera. Ciera Wilkon was a guard who worked the day shift inside the prison.

Ciera was a tall, thin woman with long lemonade braids. She had dark brown eyes and a wide smile with full lips that Randy Jr. preferred to suck on. For the first time in his life, Randy Jr. felt like he was in love with someone. Ciera Wilkon enthralled him.

Just like his night shift girlfriend, Raine, Ciera was an asset to Randy Jr. She made sure that his packages entered the prison without any interference.

Weekly, Randy Jr.'s girl Shemeika came to visit him. When she visited, she passed him the package of dope that he needed to sell throughout the prison. Randy Jr.

had the entire prison on lockdown at the moment. When he first entered the prison, he noticed that there was a shortage of supply. He quickly contacted his boy, Reggie and got things going.

Reggie Cartwright had turned out to be one of Randy Jr.'s most trusted confidants. Reggie handled all of Randy Jr.'s runs and deliveries. He kept the business running on the outside while Randy Jr. was locked up.

Reggie vowed to protect the business with his life, and Randy Jr. actually believed him. He took Reggie for his word because Reggie saved his life. Reggie protected Randy Jr. like a bodyguard. He made sure that anyone who stepped to Randy Jr. had to run through him first. He ran interference.

Randy Jr. watched Reggie beat a man to death in his honor. It happened a few weeks before he got locked up. They were hanging out in the back of a strip club, having a brief staff meeting while getting head. Randy Jr. felt that fellatio was the best way to relieve stress.

He and Reggie had worked out the details of a deal when some loser barged into the VIP lounge and tried to stop his girl from completing her services. Reggie took instant offense and cursed the dude out. Unfazed, Randy Jr. turned his back to the guy who pulled out a gun.

Reggie pulled out his pistol and ended the dude's life right there inside the club. The hoes started to get nervous, but Reggie took care of them. He quadrupled their tip and took their driver's licenses to ensure their silence.

After they buried the dead guy in their usual spot, Reggie poured lime around the body and covered it with dirt. They returned to the club that evening and continued their meeting as if nothing happened. Randy Jr. bought his boy a Maserati Ghibli to show his gratitude. He never expected someone to save his life.

Reggie was a standup guy. Reggie set the dope up for Ciera to hand deliver to Randy Jr. Ciera transported the money and the dope. She did the exchange for a mere 5% of the profit. Randy Jr. didn't mind shelling out a small amount of cash to keep money flowing through the business.

His girl Ciera was trustworthy and beautiful. Randy Jr. spent most of the day trying to get her in a room alone. Ciera was his chameleon. She could be anyone he asked for. She regularly changed her hairstyle from braids to wigs to weave, and her nails were elegantly done.

She and Randy Jr. shared many intimate moments in dark hallways and empty or abandoned classrooms. The prison was under complete surveillance, but there were some areas that even the cameras couldn't catch.

Ciera was well aware of those areas. She and Randy Jr. christened each one. Randy Jr. made sure that Ciera's pockets were laced at all times. Reggie arranged to pay her rent up for the next year, and he handed her cash each month.

She was grateful for her relationship with her new man. Ciera confided in Randy Jr. that she never met anyone like him before. Randy Jr. knew that she was correct because he knew that she was a shy woman. Ciera didn't realize her own potential. Randy Jr. knew that if she ever realized just how lovely she was, Ciera would be a force to be reckoned with.

She was only 25 years old and already had six years in at the facility. She didn't have any children and was currently pursuing a degree in Criminal Justice. Randy Jr. felt like he didn't deserve a minute of Ciera's time let alone time inside of her. That's why when she told him that she was pregnant, he didn't make her get rid of it.

He convinced her to keep the pregnancy a secret until it was absolutely necessary. Randy Jr. didn't want her to lose her job. If their relationship was exposed, she could possibly face jail time.

It didn't matter to Ciera though, she was in love with him. Randy Jr. had to keep her in line, or she would fuck up their entire game. He continued to encourage Ciera to do the right thing and continue to come to work every day as she had before.

As long as nothing changed, Randy Jr. could continue to line his pockets and Ciera's too.

Chapter 22

Spencer unlocked his front door and quickly closed the door behind him. He locked the deadbolt and chained the door. For the past several days, Spencer felt like someone was following him. After his conversation with the Detective, Spencer was spooked.

He knew that the Police would be banging down his door to arrest him soon. Spencer could still see the look of concern on the Detective's face when he advised Spencer to get an attorney. Spencer still hadn't taken his advice.

He didn't know what to do. Spencer had avoided everyone's calls. He didn't want to involve anyone in his mess. Artie already had to dispose of a decomposing mouth. Spencer knew that he was a liability to Artie's career.

It was too much for Spencer to consider, so he distanced himself for a while.

Spencer unlocked his phone and read the text messages that flooded his phone. Artie was looking for him, and so was Sidney. Sidney had a message from Spencer's mom, who had also been trying to contact him. Kandi texted him to say that she was on her way home from Cairo and wanted to get together.

Spencer wanted to call everyone back and tell them that there was a chance that they wouldn't be hearing from him for a while. He figured it would be best if he could just tell everyone what was going on in his life, but he couldn't.

His family relied on him. Spencer couldn't let them see him fail. He couldn't tell his friends that he thought that maybe he was a murderer. They would commit him to a mental institution. Spencer knew that he had to be strategic.

He opened his wine cooler door and grabbed the bottle of Merlot. After he poured himself a healthy glass of wine, Spencer took a massive gulp and collapsed on his plush leather chair. "Let's see what's going on in the world," Spencer said as he grabbed the remote control from the coffee table and turned on the television.

Spencer took another healthy sip of wine and sat his glass on the table as he flipped through the channels.

Spencer stopped when he saw Linda's picture flash across the screen. The photo was taken years before at a gala. Linda smiled brightly as her husband held her in his arms in the image on the screen.

"Police have announced that they have a person of interest in mind. Our sources say that Mr. Spencer McIntyre of Broward County is suspected in an alleged torrid love affair with Mrs. King. He saw her moments after her death," the blonde announcer said with a grim expression as an image of Spencer flashed across the screen.

"What the fuck?" Spencer asked as he noticed his Facebook profile picture splashed across the screen amongst other images from his Instagram.

"We understand that Mr. McIntyre is a fitness instructor at the 24 Hour Fitness Gym on Collins Avenue," the announcer continued spilling all of Spencer's business across the television screen as Spencer screamed in horror.

Everyone in his family was about to find out something that he just learned, he was a suspect in a murder case. Spencer finished the entire glass of wine and then grabbed the bottle from the table. He downed the smooth red liquid as he considered what his mother was thinking at the moment.

Suddenly, Spencer's cell phone began ringing. He glanced at the phone and covered his face with his hands. "Oh my gosh," he exclaimed as his mother's call went to voicemail. Seconds later a text message splashed across the screen that read, "call me, now!"

Fifteen minutes later Spencer's doorbell rang. He couldn't move to answer the door. Spencer was too drunk and weak from fright. Spencer felt helpless. This was the first time where Spencer was grateful for living alone. He was happy that no one had a key to his apartment.

Spencer figured he would lay there and continue to drown his sorrows until the morning. Artie would help him figure a way out of it all.

Spencer nearly fell to the floor when he opened his eyes to find three Police Officers standing in his house. "How did you get in here?" Spencer asked. "We knocked and announced," Officer Brimm said as he pointed to the two SWAT officers behind him.

Spencer shrugged with drunken sadness. "Spencer McIntyre we have here a warrant to search the premises," Officer Brimm stated as he handed Spencer the thick envelope labeled, "Warrant" for his review.

"You can vacate the premises if you like. We will be a while," Officer Brimm stated as Spencer scurried out of his own apartment. Once Spencer reached the hallway, he noticed several additional officers entering the building. "What's going on in there?" one of his neighbors asked as they peaked their head out of their door.

When their eyes met Spencer's they gasped in fright and quickly slammed the door behind them. Spencer could hear the locks and chains being engaged inside the apartment.

Once he reached the outdoor air, Spencer ran to his car, only to find that it was sitting on top of a tow truck bed. "What in the world?" he asked as another officer passed by him on their way to Spencer's apartment.

Spencer just began walking as he pulled out his phone and dialed Sidney's number.

"Sid...neeeyyyyy," Spencer cried into the phone as he collapsed to the ground outside his apartment building, "answer your phone, I need your help now!" Spencer placed the phone to his chest after leaving the message for Sidney and continued to cry, praying his message went through.

Chapter 23

Sidney busied herself inside her office as she prepared for her next case. She spent her first week on the job reviewing old cases. As she scanned through the files, Sidney felt a sensation of pride. She was finally doing what she wanted to do.

Her mind was all over the place. She contacted one of her instructors from the FBI Academy for assistance. Dr. Aaron Streeter was one of the top criminal profilers in the FBI. When he retired from his position, the Bureau couldn't afford to lose him or his knowledge base.

He was offered a tenured position inside the Academy. An older Black gentleman with a thick salt and pepper beard and deep penetrating eyes that made Dr. Streeter a hot item at the Academy. A lot of the female students teased about trying to seduce the older man.

They claimed that they were attracted to his physically fit body and handsome face, but Sidney knew the truth. They were drawn to Dr. Streeter's impeccably clear sense of wisdom and knowledge. Sidney witnessed it first hand when she sat in his class.

The students were enthralled by his experience and knowledge. He also had the smoothest, sexiest deep voice that sent chills up Sidney's spine. She was grateful for the opportunity to know and study under Dr. Streeter. Sidney became his protégé.

She studied his reports and reviewed his case studies for discussions in class. Dr. Streeter took a liking to Sidney. She confided in Dr. Streeter the real reason why she wanted to become an investigator. Sidney wanted to bring her father's killers to justice. Dr. Streeter sympathized with Sidney's plight.

That was the reason why she contacted him for assistance.

Dr. Streeter returned her call the same day. He was aware of Sidney's situation with her father, and apologized for not returning her previous call. He explained that they were in finals week at the academy.

When he heard her voice on the phone, the tone in his voice instantly brightened. "Sidney, how are you?" he asked as she quickly filled him in on her life since she graduated from the Academy.

"I often think about my top student," he bragged with a chuckle. Sidney was proud of her designation. She worked hard and studied even harder. When she graduated, Sidney's Grade Point Average was the highest in her class.

Sidney was on her way to the top, and Dr. Streeter knew it.

"What can I do for you?" Dr. Streeter asked, quickly getting to the point of the conversation. "I need your help," Sidney stated as she explained her current position.

"I need to identify the officers on a Police Report. I only have their badge numbers," she confessed as he listened quietly. "I don't want to alert anyone in the MPD that I am researching an old case," she added.

"I see," he said. "So, you figured since I have access to the Federal CJIS system that I will locate the information for you," he surmised. Sidney held her breath as she waited for him to decide if he would help her.

"Send me the info. I'll see what I can do," Dr. Streeter said quickly as she sighed in relief. "Thank you for helping me," she said, happily. "There's one more thing," Sidney added as Dr. Streeter laughed. Sidney was one of his favorite students.

"I need you to look into Marcus Mystic," she said quickly. Dr. Streeter didn't immediately respond so Sidney began her brief explanation about a whirlwind relationship and the scene that unfolded at Randy Jr's. visitation. Dr. Streeter was understanding and sympathetic to Sidney's situation. Just as she figured, he didn't judge or question her, he just listened.

Sidney was used to opening up to Dr. Streeter. He proved to be a trustworthy friend during some of her darkest times in the academy. There were times when Sidney struggled with her purpose, especially when she received a negative assessment or failed an exam. Dr. Streeter was always there to remind Sidney that she wasn't doing the work in vain.

She gave Dr. Streeter the abridged version of her love story, omitting Vondra amongst other things. Dr. Streeter listened as she blurted out the last of her story then he let out a long sigh. "Sidney, I'll take care of it," he assured to her delight. She thanked him profusely.

"Anything I can do to help you, Sidney, you know I will do it. I have a class coming in so I have to let you go, dear," he said as they ended their call with promises to meet up again, soon.

Sidney was on her way to getting some real answers. She glanced at her phone as it vibrated loudly on the desk. Mystic was calling her again. Sidney watched as the call ended and went to voicemail. Several seconds later her phone indicated that she had another voicemail.

Sidney pressed the trash icon on the phone and deleted the message without listening to it, just as she had done many times before. Sidney wasn't ready to talk to Mystic until she found out the truth.

She heard a knock on the door. "Come in," she announced as Kimberly Shields sauntered slowly inside the room. Kimberly was her new secretary. "How are you doing Kim?" Sidney asked as Kim feigned a smile. "I will survive Ms. Sidney," she said quietly as she placed another manila folder on her desk.

Sidney glanced over at the stack of folders already on her desk, awaiting her review. She was told in her morning meeting with her superior that they were working through their backlog of cases now that she was on board. It made Sidney feel needed and valued to have so much work to do, but her mind was elsewhere.

Once Kimberly left her office, Sidney opened her black leather briefcase and retrieved the Police Report. She took a picture of the report with her phone and texted Dr. Streeter the image.

Dr. Streeter immediately responded with a thumbs up. Sidney prayed that he would help her find her father's killers. If anyone could help her, she knew that Dr. Streeter could. Sidney wanted to ask Garcia about the names on the Police Report, but she had trouble reaching him.

For some strange reason, her calls went directly to voicemail. She left messages requesting that Garcia return her calls, but she didn't hear from him. Sidney was growing concerned. Garcia was behaving strangely lately. Sidney didn't know what to think about anyone, anymore. Everyone had a surprise up their sleeves.

Ten minutes later, there was a knock on her door. Her Superior, Darrion King, was holding a file with a stern look on his face. "Here is our next case to profile," he said. "This is an interesting case. The culprit murdered six people so far in rural Virginia. We are looking to find out more about her so we can pinpoint her current location," he explained.

Anna Kingston was a mother of three and a victim of bipolar disorder. She was also Sidney's newest case to review. Sidney read the workup about her latest case.

Anna was found standing over her husband's mutilated body one balmy September evening. Anna was given bail based on her father's connections as a judge.

That didn't stop Anna from jumping bail nine days later. She eluded capture for over nine years, so far. Sidney stared at the last known image of Anna with determination. "Don't worry you won't be able to run too much longer," Sidney assured herself as she tossed the case file aside and continued logging her cold cases.

Chapter 24

Mystic sat in his office chair and leaned back with his arms behind his head. He needed a vacation, desperately. His last meeting for the day just ended, and he was ready to go home and unwind. He needed a cigar and a glass of scotch. Mystic was tired and was at the beginning stages of a nervous breakdown. He was coming apart.

His wife was calling him nonstop. It was to the point where he couldn't turn his phone on any longer. Mystic couldn't take it anymore. He wanted to just run away from it all.

Sidney still wasn't taking his calls. He tried to give her time to settle down, but Mystic worried that she would forget about him by the time he was ready to tell her everything.

He knew that he had her heart. She gave him all of her that night before they found Randy Jr. Sidney loved him just as much as he loved her. He took solace in knowing that. It would just take a while longer for him to convince Sidney that he genuinely had her best interests in mind.

His ringing office phone interrupted his thoughts. He smiled as he imagined his sexy secretary's smiling face on the other end of the phone. "Yes, dear," he asked as she giggled on the phone. He teased her about being his office wife.

She made sure that he had lunch every day. His secretary took care of his dry cleaning, his schedule, and his vehicle's maintenance. Mystic was happy about the perks that came along with the job of Chief of Police.

Although Mystic would never admit it, all of the treatment made him feel like the Mayor. Now, that was his ultimate goal. Mystic always wanted to become a political figure. What better place to be a Mayor than in Miami?

Sadly, Mystic knew that his chances were now slim of even remaining a Police Chief. Once someone began to scratch the surface of his façade, it would all come tumbling down. That was his fear.

"I have a call from Vera for you," his secretary added with a smile. Mystic's blood ran completely cold. How did his aunt get ahold of his phone number at work?

Mystic wondered what Vondra got into that warranted a phone call in his office.

He cleared his throat and responded, "thank you, Dear. I'll take it," he said as he waited for his secretary to hang up the phone. When he said, "Hello?" Vera immediately began speaking.

"Marcus you are in danger!" Vera exclaimed. Marcus chuckled at his aunt's revelation. "I know Auntie. Everyone is out to get me," he confessed with a chuckle as he waited for her to laugh along with him. When she didn't laugh, his heart rate increased.

"What do you mean?" he asked as she started babbling.

"Vondra escaped! No one knows where she is, but she killed three of our staff members and a patient before she left. The North Florida Police Department have been here interviewing people. They put out a BOLO for Vondra. Mystic she is crazy and heading your way," Vera yelled into the phone as Marcus clenched the phone in his hand, dumbfounded.

Mystic mouthed the words, Be On The Lookout (BOLO) as images of his deranged wife flashed through his mind. His heart pounded with fear while Vera continued explaining the carnage that Vondra left in her wake, this time.

"Are you sure?" he asked calmly, while Vera screamed for him to run as far as he could from Vondra. "Damnit, Marcus! Why would I lie to you? I've been trying to reach you. I don't know where she's heading, but I ask that you please, please be safe," Vera begged as Marcus assured her that he would be careful.

He asked his aunt for prayer before she hung up the phone. After she said her prayer, Mystic thanked her and hung up with his heart pounding in his chest and his palms sweaty. Mystic didn't realize that his entire face was wet with perspiration.

Vondra was loose. She was still out there killing people. Mystic didn't know what to do. He needed protection, but how did the Chief of Police secure a Police detail, without telling everyone that his wife was insane and a killer?

Chapter 25

Sidney completed her final case of the day and let out an exhausted sigh. She loved her new job, but the backlog of work left by her predecessor seemed like an insurmountable task.

She was grateful to make some headway with her work. After she placed the completed file in her outgoing bin, she began to pack her things for the evening. Her day was finally over.

Sidney drove along the highway when her cellphone rang. The fright in Spencer's voice made her blood run cold. Something was seriously wrong with her friend, and she was going to find out exactly what it was.

Sidney pulled up to the curb just like Spencer instructed her on the phone. "Get in!" she advised as she pulled up close to him. Spencer took one look at Sidney and wanted to cry for her. She looked like she had been through her own form of hell. "Are you alright?" he asked as Sidney simply nodded.

Spencer looked around for one final time and then climbed inside the car. When Spencer collapsed inside her vehicle, Sidney looked at him like he was crazy. He had a wild look in his eyes, and his face was bright red.

"What's going on, Spencer?" Sidney asked as she drove off from the corner. "Sidney, did you see the news?" Spencer asked. Sidney told him that she hadn't been home since earlier that morning. "This caseload has been insane. I've been stuck inside the office for the entire day. I just got off from work," Sidney said as she pointed to her work clothes that she was wearing, "and I'm looking now at the message you left."

"Sidney, I'm a suspect in a murder," Spencer blurted out as Sidney swerved the car in surprise. The owner of the vehicle in the opposite lane laid on their horn in response.

Sidney didn't notice, she was still digesting what her best friend just confessed. "Murder? Who? When? Why? Spencer, I don't believe you," Sidney rambled as Spencer began to weep.

Sidney stared at her friend in confusion. She pulled over to the side of the road and took Spencer in her arms as he cried.

"I don't know what happened, Sid. One minute I'm partying with you guys the next I wake up in bed at Steven and Linda's house. I think I was drugged, but I can't find a way to prove it, Sidney," Spencer explained as Sidney listened with her mouth hanging agape. I should have just left when you guys did!

"So did you see Steven kill his wife?" she asked as Spencer shook his head. "No! I didn't see anything. All I remember is Linda's dead body. Now Steven is stalking me. He's sending me letters with pictures from that night. Sidney, I think he's trying to frame me for his wife's murder!" Spencer cried.

Sidney digested his words with sadness. "Okay, I know of a great attorney in the area. I will have him come to see you in the morning. You can stay with us tonight," Sidney announced. "Sidney, are you sure that your mother will be comfortable with me staying in your house?" he asked.

Sidney considered Spencer's question. Florence would curse her daughter out if she brought Spencer inside the house to stay. It wasn't because he was a suspected murderer, but the fact that he and Sidney were not married.

Florence wouldn't have any shacking up inside her home. Sidney was sure of it.

"On second thought," Sidney suggested. "I'll get you a room at the Westin," Sidney announced as Spencer smiled at her. "You're so sweet Sidney," Spencer responded as Sidney drove in the direction of the hotel on the waterfront.

She figured that Spencer would benefit from a nice view of a beautiful hotel for now. She needed to get home and get some rest. Sidney couldn't wait to take a hot shower and climb in her bed.

Chapter 26

Spencer lay in the bed with his cell phone on silent. He knew that eventually, he would need to contact his family and tell them that he was alive. Spencer finally bit the bullet and dialed his mother's phone number.

His mother answered the phone on the first ring. There was no way he could hide from her any longer.

"Spencer, that pretty girl from Channel 7 news... Haven Rey said that you were wanted on suspicion of murder, son. What is going on? Where have you been? Are you safe? Do you need help?" she asked.

His mother bombarded him with questions that Spencer couldn't answer.

"Mom, I don't know what's going on," he confessed. "I got myself in a situation, and I don't know how to get out of it. I have a meeting with my attorney later this afternoon. As soon as I know what he wants me to do, I will call you and let you know. Don't worry, Mama. I would never hurt anyone. The truth will come out soon," Spencer assured his mother and himself at the same time.

"Please tell Dad that I am fine and I will let him know something as soon as I hear from my attorney," Spencer advised. "Mama, don't believe anything that you see on the television. I'm not in jail. I'm just chilling at a hotel for now. Please don't watch the news," he pleaded as she assured him that she would listen to his advice.

Spencer hung up the phone with his mother and decided to get dressed to meet his defense attorney.

Spencer didn't have any clothes to change into, so he took a brief shower and dressed in the clothes that he wore earlier that day. Spencer didn't want to return to his house, because he was afraid of what he might find.

It killed him to watch the Police tear through his house. Spencer didn't want to return to his home and find a mess. He would have broken down, and he couldn't take that emotional drama before his meeting.

His attorney met him in the restaurant across the street from his hotel. Spencer walked to the restaurant feeling uneasy about his meeting.

As he walked down the street he noticed that people stared at him out of curiosity or fear, he couldn't tell the difference. Some people stared at him as if they recognized him, then hurried away from him, quickly.

Spencer wondered if he should've gone outside wearing a disguise. When he entered the restaurant, the host stared at him like he was garbage. "May I help you?" he asked with a stiff upper lip.

"Yes, I'm meeting someone here, Isaac Stein," he said as the host walked him through the restaurant to the seating in the back. When he saw Isaac, Spencer smiled with surprise. Isaac looked nothing like he expected.

Isaac Spencer was a tall, physically fit guy who looked like he was fresh out of law school.

"Spencer McIntyre? I'm Isaac," he said with a firm handshake and a smile that met his eyes. Spencer sat down, and they ordered their drinks and lunch. While they waited for their food to arrive, Spencer filled Isaac in on the basics behind his case.

Isaac listened to Spencer without saying a word. He let Spencer ramble on throughout the entire luncheon. After a while, Spencer wanted to inquire if Isaac understood what he was saying. Isaac slowly wiped at his mouth with his linen napkin and responded. "Of course Mr. McIntyre. I understand exactly what you're saying, and I believe that I can help you," he said. "I think you made the right choice by contacting me early. It is best to get in front of these things, so they don't become an issue down the line. I hate surprises," Isaac confessed with a fake laugh.

Spencer crossed his fingers as Isaac spoke. "How will we handle your payment? I am currently unemployed," Spencer confessed as Isaac waved his hand.

"I am doing this as a favor for a dear friend. You concern yourself with getting me all of the information that I requested so we can work on clearing your name. I want to see the images within the shoebox and everything that Linda's husband has mailed or delivered to you," he said as Spencer thought about the package containing Linda's mouth.

He decided not to mention the package. He knew for a fact that Garcia got rid of the package so it wouldn't come back to bite them both later.

Spencer listened intently as Isaac unveiled his tentative plan for Spencer's defense, should it come to that point. He was thrilled with his meeting with Isaac. Spencer walked back to the hotel wearing a bright smile. It didn't matter to Spencer that people stopped and pointed at him as he walked around.

Everyone saw the news reports.

Chapter 27

Vondra pulled up to the house and glanced at the mailbox. The numbers on the mailbox read 8210. She couldn't believe it. After all of this time, she was back at square one.

Vondra finally made it. After what felt like a month of driving and weeks inside of hotel room after hotel room, she was finally there.

Vondra checked her reflection in the mirror and smiled at what she saw. "Elsa, I'm here," she sang as she climbed out of Lawrences' vehicle. Vondra was grateful that she chose to steal Lawrence's car from the mental hospital parking lot. It was a reliable vehicle. Vondra smoothed her brand new Banana Republic sweater over her jeans as she sashayed to the front door.

Vondra patted the side of her purse to ensure that her gun was still resting inside, just waiting to be used. She couldn't wait to put a bullet between her sister's eyes. She loved her sister, Elsa, but it was time for Elsa to meet her demise. Vondra took in the sights and sounds of the neighborhood. She wanted to absorb it all because this would be her last time there.

She could see the original white paint poking through the shutters and vents of the house. The house held so many beautiful and traumatic memories. Vondra was tormented by the images that flooded her mind just by standing in the yard.

Vondra sacrificed too much for her sister's sake. She gave away too much for Elsa. It was now time for Elsa to pay it forward.

She couldn't believe that after all these years apart, her sister would relocate and move to their childhood home. What would make Elsa want to live in the house where all of their trauma began? Vondra wondered about her sister's sanity as she approached the steps.

She took the safety off her gun before she exited her car. Vondra placed the gun in her hand already cocked and unlocked.

Vondra was prepared for anything.

Vondra slowly walked towards the front door and looked around the white porch. She remembered being a young girl, jumping and playing on the porch all day. She recalled playing with her sister Elsa in the front yard while their mother watched them, sipping lemonade from the porch swing.

It was a lovely existence if it wasn't for her abusive father. Vondra's blood boiled as she thought about her father. He pissed her off the way he treated them. Vondra stared at the front yard. Who would have known the horrors that they suffered inside the house with the well manicured front yard?

Vondra walked up the heavy steps and opened the screen door. Once the screen door cracked open, Vondra knocked softly on the door. She waited for someone to answer, but no one came to the door.

Finally, she decided to bang on the door to get some attention. Vondra pounded and banged on the door as she waited for someone to open it. She knew that someone was inside because she could hear the television in the background.

Vondra walked around the side of the house. She scanned the basement for an open window, the top one that always had the broken lock. She placed the gun back in her purse, lifted the window open and climbed inside the house.

Once inside the house, Vondra slowly walked around searching for Elsa. When she reached the top of the stairs, Vondra pulled out her gun and opened the basement door that led towards the upstairs of the house.

There she saw her sister lounging on the couch; or better yet, passed out. Resting on the hardwood floor sat an empty bottle of Vodka. Vondra resisted the urge to smother her sister with the pillow; instead, she began to put her plan in action, as she placed her gun back in her purse, she ran upstairs and removed her clothes. Vondra walked inside Elsa's room and opened the closet door. She quickly rifled through the clothes, then stopped suddenly.

Vondra smiled with glee when she noticed the waitress uniform on the cheap wire hanger. The pink uniform had white ruffles on the sleeves and hemline. The name tag on the uniform bore Elsa's name. Vondra tossed on the uniform. She was grateful that her sister maintained her weight, because it fit perfectly.

She stood in the full length mirror appraising her image. For a moment, she was startled by her own reflection. "Elsa?" Vondra questioned her reflection with a smile. Satisfied with her image she crept slowly down the stairs.

When she stepped inside the living room, she was relieved to find her sister, still asleep on the couch. Vondra tapped her on the shoulder and waited patiently for Elsa's eyes to focus on her.

When Elsa opened her eyes she had to blink several times to be sure that she wasn't looking at her own reflection. It didn't take long for Elsa's memory to register, however. She suddenly realized who she was staring at and screamed bloody murder. "Get away from me!" Elsa screeched jumping up from the couch. "How'd you get in here? And why are you wearing my uniform?" she demanded as Vondra slowly approached her sister.

The two women began to fight like never before. Vondra hit Elsa with all of her might, sending her flying into the curio cabinet. She screamed as all of her knick-knacks fell crashing to the floor behind her.

Elsa charged at Vondra, but she wasn't quick enough. Vondra ducked and grabbed her sister by her hair.

"Time's up, Elsa!" Vondra declared as she grabbed her sister by the throat and squeezed hard. Elsa's face turned beet red as she coughed and struggled to breathe. Sensing the pain on her face, Vondra released her grasp.

Elsa coughed and gagged as she struggled to catch her breath. Moving towards the couch, she grabbed her cell phone and turned to face her sister. "You're too late, Vondra. The FBI was alerted when you escaped. I'm sure someone is watching my house right now," she said with a smug grin. "In fact...hello...I need help," Elsa whispered into the cell phone mouthpiece, staring directly at her sister.

Vondra looked at her sister and frowned as she considered her options. She could run and try her luck at being an escapee, or she could face this situation head-on for the last time.

"I love you, sis, but it's time for me to live happily ever after," Vondra declared. Suddenly there was a knock at the door. Vondra and Elsa both stopped fighting to stare at the door. Vondra looked at Elsa and coaxed her to the door. "It's your damn house. Answer the door," she instructed her sister.

The moment she opened the door, she was tackled to the ground. "Vondra Duncan Mystic you are under arrest for breaking and entering and the murders of several employees at the North Florida Mental Hospital," the FBI Agent announced as they handcuffed her.

"It's all over now. You can leave my son and me alone!" she said as Vondra squirmed and fought against the restraints trying to get at her sister.

"I've been running from her for my entire life. She tried to kill me when I was nine, and she never stopped trying. I swear I can't believe that it's been nearly six years and you are still acting like this Vondra?" Elsa questioned.

"What did I ever do to you?" she asked as she stood and stared her sister eye to eye.

Vondra glared at her sister, Elsa. She wanted to scratch the bitch's eyes out. Vondra wore a sinister grin on her face as she listened to her sister rant.

"You stole the only man I ever loved!" Vondra screamed. Elsa looked at Vondra as if she were speaking a different language. Then she finally spoke as she waved her hand at the Federal Officers. "Please just take her away. This is all too much for us to bare," she said as the Officers nodded their acceptance and dragged Vondra out of the house screaming.

"You got the wrong person. Please just listen to me!" Vondra screamed as the FBI Agents dragged her to the car and placed her in the backseat.

After the FBI Agents took Vondra out to their car, Elsa stood at the window and stared at her sister. She was so happy that her sister would finally be out of her life.

She couldn't wait to begin her new life of freedom without the threats of her sister. Elsa smiled at Vondra as they dragged her away. "You can scream all you want, sis, they'll never hear you," she said laughing to herself.

Chapter 28

Spencer heard Artie's voice in his head as he entered the gym. Artie reminded Spencer to continue on with his life as if nothing was going on. His attorney had the same advice for him. "Spencer, you have not committed a crime. Do not behave as if you have. I will work on building your defense," he volunteered. "But you need to work on maintaining the same life you had before this incident with Linda and Steven," he advised.

At first, Spencer wasn't going to return to his job, but as his attorney advised, Spencer wasn't under arrest.

When he left his meeting with Isaac, Spencer felt like he was walking on air. Isaac had Spencer fired up to sue the Police department for leaking his name as a possible suspect.

According to his attorney, it was worth a shot.

Spencer didn't care about getting money from anyone, he just wanted his life back. His mother called him daily, sometimes three or four times per day about the case.

She wanted to know what Spencer's plans were. Really, she wanted Spencer to explain everything to her, but he absolutely refused. Spencer's family wasn't fully aware of his flamboyant lifestyle. While they all knew that he was gay no one expected Spencer to be as free as he was sexually. Spencer rarely maintained long relationships; instead he opted for one night stands and less complicated situations.

None of these situations did he feel comfortable breaking down to his 67-year-old mother. Spencer simply told his mother to put his name on the altar at the next Sunday service. She assured him that she prayed for all of her wayward children, which made Spencer feel extra special.

Spencer walked inside the gym and bounced to the beat of the music playing overhead. He didn't notice the stares and diverted glances that were shot his way.

Spencer didn't care about any of that. He just had to access the box that was located in his locker. That box would be his only evidence of stalking according to his attorney. If Spencer could prove that Steven was stalking him, he would be home free.

He hoped that his attorney could help clear his name using that shoebox.

"Hey, Spencer is everything okay?" Stephanie asked as she followed Spencer back to his office. "We've heard some bizarre things, Spencer," Stephanie continued following Spencer until he suddenly stopped and turned to face her.

"Stephanie, can I help you?" Spencer asked in a perturbed manner. "I was just wondering if you were alright. The Police showed up here a few hours ago and searched the building," she advised and then quickly walked away.

Spencer's heartbeat quickened at the mere mention of the Police. He wondered why they were searching through his things at work? It bothered Spencer that the Police were basically accusing him of murder in front of the entire world.

His friends and family looked at him like he was a monster. Spencer wondered when it would all end. As he accessed the swim area, he said a prayer, hoping that his locker was still intact.

The minute he reached the locker area, Spencer knew that his luck had just run out. The lock on his personal locker was hanging loosely on the cabinet. When Spencer opened the door to the locker and revealed emptiness, he screamed.

Spencer was finally at the end of his rope.

He couldn't figure a way out of the mess he found himself in. Spencer quickly turned around and walked out of the gym in frustration. He had to leave town or figure out a way to pin the murder on Steven because as it seemed at the moment, Spencer was their only suspect.

The sudden thought of his predicament sent Spencer reeling. He walked to the front of the gym, his head throbbing and body sweating profusely. He could barely find his way to the door as he stumbled exiting the gym, possible for the last time.

Chapter 29

Sidney sipped on a glass of wine as she anxiously picked at the dinner roll on the table in front of her. She didn't know why she accepted the dinner invitation. Part of her needed to get out of the house, while the other part wanted to enjoy an expensive dinner at a fancy restaurant.

She glanced across the table at Darrell Harper. A tall, handsome man in his late 40s, Darrell, had dark features and a bright white smile. He sported a full beard and a head full of soft, salt and pepper, more pepper than salt curls. He was an exquisite man and a sharp dresser.

Darrell took Sidney's hand in his and smiled at her. "Sidney, I'm so happy that you agreed to have dinner with me," he said with a twinkle in his eye. Sidney smiled back as they dined and chatted about life.

He filled Sidney in on the updates of his own life. Darrell Harper had a long-standing career with the FBI, and was one of Sidney's mentors while in the academy, but lately, he was trying his hand at writing. Sidney listened intently as he described to her the plot behind his first book.

She was happy to have a distraction from Mystic and also grateful to have Darrell on her side. He told her that he would do anything that she needed regarding the case involving Mystic.

Sidney was intrigued by Darrell. He was handsome, funny and well educated. Darrell was from a small town in Minnesota. He still had family there, but his parents passed on many years prior. He didn't have any children, but he was active in raising his niece and nephew after while his sister was deployed to Germany in the US Air Force.

After filling the air with talk about his past life and current dreams, Darrell folded his arms and leaned forward. "Sidney, I would like to talk to you about the information that you requested," he said as she leaned in to listen.

"I promise that I will find you anything that I can, but you must remain discreet. You are planning to look into something that could possibly bring harm your way. I just want you to remember that the Police will do anything to protect their own," he advised as she nodded.

"They will have met their match with you, however," he added as she smiled. "You remind me of my niece. I just want you to be careful," he added.

To ease the tension that had grown in the air, Darrell began to quiz Sidney about her current job duties. Sidney didn't want to talk about her job but welcomed the change of conversation.

She loved her work history. Being a Psychologist was a goal that she couldn't wait to achieve, but Sidney felt like she was missing something. The excitement from her time in the FBI Academy spoiled her. Once she returned to the office, things began to settle down, and she became bored.

Sidney would never complain, however. She was grateful for her job. It helped her support her mother's efforts in paying the bills and providing for them. However, Sidney had to admit that she was beginning to feel burned out with her caseload. The cold cases were stacking up on her desk, and she was starting to feel the pressure.

She was ready to review new cases. Sidney had new ideas and techniques that she intended on offering to the Bureau, but she needed an opportunity to shine to make it happen.

Her love life put more pressure on her than her career. No matter what she did, her mind remained on Mystic. Sidney still shuddered when she thought about their time together. She lost herself in Mystic's arms as he made her body tremble in places she never knew existed.

Mystic was gentle and loving the entire time, but Sidney couldn't stop thinking about those moments when he gave her all he had. Mystic had Sidney's legs on his shoulder as he explored places deep within her. Sidney couldn't move, her body was in a paralyzed trance as Mystic kissed, licked and lost himself inside her.

Sidney fell in love with Mystic all over again that night. She wished that it could have lasted forever. Darrell told Sidney that he would need to enlist the help of Dr. Streeter, who also knew and adored Sidney from the FBI academy, with her request. She happily agreed as Darrell continued talking, but Sidney couldn't hear him speak.

Sidney felt terrible for checking out of their conversation, but she just couldn't sit there any longer.

Sidney excused herself from the table and went directly to the bathroom. Once she opened the doors, the cool breeze from the ventilation system sent her hair flying all around her face. Sidney walked inside and headed towards the white porcelain sinks to splash water on her face. "Get it together, Sid," she chastised. Sidney was frustrated with herself. She tried not to think about Mystic, but he had been on her mind for weeks.

Mystic tried to contact her, but after several ignored texts and calls he finally took the hint. Sidney wasn't ready to deal with Mystic, and she was grateful that he finally decided to give her the space she needed to process things.

Although she tried to ignore him and throw herself into her work, Sidney still couldn't keep her mind off of Mystic. He was in her dreams. Mystic's muscular body and massive arms made her body quiver. She had to get to the bottom of the situation with Mystic and her Brother. Sidney knew that sooner or later she would need to speak with him about the night she lost her father.

She really didn't want to admit it, but Sidney was afraid. She was scared that Mystic would say something that would forever change the way she saw him. Sidney was afraid that Mystic would make her hate him.

Using the tissues in the fancy gold leaf box, Sidney wiped her face. She took one last look in the mirror and headed out of the bathroom. "Get it together," she repeated to herself. It was a lovely evening, and she enjoyed spending time being wined and dined. She was also enjoying the distraction that her mentor Darrell Harper caused.

All she had to do was keep her mind on her evening and off Mystic. It was a tricky thing. She could only see Mystic.

That's when she realized, Mystic was standing in front of her.

Sidney blinked twice and stared with her mouth open as Mystic gently grabbed her by the arms and kissed her. She tried her best to resist his kiss, but it was pointless. She wanted him to kiss her more than he wanted to.

Sidney was head over heels in love with him.

"Sidney, I've missed you so much. You're all I think about," he whispered to her as he held her hands in his. Sidney looked around the back of the restaurant to ensure that no one was around. When she realized that the restroom section was empty, she spoke. "Mystic, there is so much going on in my head. I don't know what to say to you," she confessed.

"Sidney, I didn't do anything that night. I didn't touch your father," he confessed quickly. "So you were there?" Sidney asked her eyes narrowed peering deep into his green eyes.

"I wasn't there, Sidney. I didn't do anything to your father. Your brother is mistaken!" he exclaimed as Sidney stared into his eyes, searching for a lie.

"I know that you're here with someone," he said as he glanced down at the floor. "Call me when you get home,

Sidney," he said as she nodded. "Okay," she said as he leaned forward to steal another kiss from her.

Suddenly, his cell phone rang as Sidney walked away.

Chapter 30

Mystic walked out of the restaurant feeling like a million bucks. He felt victorious for being able to get through to Sidney. She was a stubborn woman. Nearly a month had passed since they spent time together and he missed her, dearly.

He could still taste her soft lips. Mystic loved Sidney, and he prayed for an opportunity to reach out to her. Sidney didn't understand how much she really meant to him.

After he got rid of Vondra, he expected to be able to spend more time with Sidney. It bothered him that Sidney's brother had to fuck up his game. Mystic replayed that morning in his head, repeatedly.

Randy Jr. lunged forward calling him a coward. If only they knew how much he did to save them, they would have thanked him. Mystic pleaded with the Police Officers that evening. They wanted to arrest Florence for impeding with an arrest, but he talked them out of it. He comforted Sidney and Randy Jr. and convinced his comrades to take Randy Sr. to the hospital when he noticed the injuries to his face and body.

How would he have known that the injuries Randy Sr. sustained in the apartment that evening would have led to his death? Mystic replayed that night and so many others, often. That was one of the reasons why he preferred to sip on a glass of Scotch late in the evenings.

It was the only thing that relaxed him. Especially since he didn't have Sidney to lean on. Mystic felt like he was going crazy without Sidney. Nothing made sense to him, anymore.

The one time he received what he was asking for, he found himself on the brink of losing his career, his love, and his mind. Mystic wished that there was someone he could blame for his misfortune, but he knew that it was all his fault.

Finally, after years of getting by on his charm and good looks, his chickens were coming home to roost. Mystic would ultimately have to face the issues that he hid from so masterfully.

The thought made his head ache. As he rubbed his head, he continued to sprint towards his car. He figured that would be his safest place to unwind and think for a minute. He needed a minute of quiet so he could collect his thoughts.

Once he reached his black Tahoe, Mystic unlocked the door and climbed inside. His phone vibrated, alerting him to a new voicemail message. His heart pounded with anxiety as he wiped at his wet brow. Mystic realized that he was coming undone. He had to get himself together before he lost it all.

Mystic glanced at his phone and sighed loudly. His Aunt Vera was still trying to reach him. Mystic knew that she was only checking on him to ensure his safety, but he couldn't talk to her at the moment. He loved his aunt, but he couldn't deal with all of her drama at the moment.

If he were honest, he would admit that he was angry with his Aunt Vera. Mystic couldn't believe that he entrusted her with Vondra, and Vondra still escaped.

Vera was one of the most accomplished charge nurses in the field. She was one of the best. Mystic felt uneasy about the fact that Vondra was able to trick someone as skilled as Vera.

It also didn't help that Vondra was still killing people. Mystic figured that she would have been on her best behavior in a mental facility. The last time he committed her to a mental health facility, she turned herself around, completely.

Vondra spent three months inside the mental health facility at Florida Medical Center. He visited her often, and he saw a significant improvement in his wife. After three months, Vondra was released, and she remained on her best behavior until he met Sidney.

That was when things began to unravel again.

Chapter 31

Spencer placed the instructions for the overnight trainer on his desk and locked the office door. As he approached his car a sinking feeling hit him in the pit of his stomach. Spencer looked around quickly. It felt like someone was watching him, but he quickly brushed it off.

He got in the car, and Joe's smooth voice began to sing about love. He turned the radio up as he backed out of the parking space. All of a sudden, tires screeched, and a horn blared loudly causing Spencer to slam on his brakes.

As he looked up, both hands gripped on the steering wheel, Steven swerved from behind him. Spencer screamed as Steven drove slowly past him pointing his fingers as if he was shooting a gun. Spencer watched with his mouth hanging open as Steven slowly drove away.

Spencer sat frozen in his seat for nearly ten minutes. He couldn't move all he could think about was Steven and Linda. Spencer reached for his phone but began to panic when he couldn't find it. Suddenly a loud horn blared as drivers started to yell at him. At that moment, Spencer looked up and realized that he was in the middle of the road. Drivers yelled out their car windows for him to get out of the middle of the road.

Embarrassed by the entire spectacle and anxiety-ridden, Spencer sat in the car with his hands over his ears.

Spencer began to cry uncontrollably and just couldn't function. A Police Officer drove by and noticed the stalled vehicle. The Officer pulled up behind him and turned his lights on. He got out of his patrol vehicle, walked up to the window and noticed Spencer with his hands covering his ears. The Officer tapped on the window to get Spencer's attention.

The Officer's sudden appearance startled Spencer, causing a complete anxiety attack.

"Officer, I need to talk to someone, I just can't do this anymore!" Spencer yelled, crying uncontrollably. The officer asked him to step out of the vehicle and place his hands on the top of the trunk.

Determined to get it all off his chest, Spencer began to blurt out his words, "I have to tell somebody now," Spencer said in a soft broken voice.

Spencer's resolve crumbled as he collapsed into tears. Spencer was placed in the back of the Police car. The Officer gave Spencer the option of leaving his car on the side of the road by signing a waiver or having it towed. Spencer signed the waiver.

The Officer moved the car to the side of the road, and locked the doors, leaving a copy of the signed waiver in the door jam. He then cuffed and searched Spencer before situating him inside of his patrol car before driving off. "So should I read you your rights now, or should I wait until we get to the station?" asked Officer Brimm.

Officer Brimm recalled what Spencer uttered on the side of the road and considered reading Spencer his rights immediately. He began to read Spencer his rights, but Spencer cut him off, "I just can't do this anymore, I'm tired and I just can't, I don't know what I did." Spencer sobbed.

Officer Brimm listened to Spencer ramble and advised him gently, "Don't say anything else, anything you say can and will be used against you in a court of law." Officer Brimm continued to read Spencer his rights as Spencer sobbed quietly in the back seat.

"Do you understand what I just told you, sir?" Officer Brimm asked. "Yes Officer, I understand!" Spencer said as he lowered his head, trying to wipe the tears off of his face. Officer Brimm accelerated after telling the dispatcher that he would be en route to the station with one black male.

The ride was rather soothing for Spencer. He laid his head back on the seat, and went into deep thought, trying to figure out what he was going to say when he arrived at the station. He had no idea if he killed Linda, or if Steven killed his wife. All Spencer knew was that he was covered with her blood when he found her in the kitchen. He couldn't for the life of him remember what happened the night before.

Artie hid the box with the mouth in it and told Spencer that he would take care of everything. Spencer was so grateful for the way Artie took charge of everything. He just remembered being embraced by the love of his life the day the mouth came to the house from UPS. Did Artie know what was going on? Spencer slowly closed his eyes and just continued to enjoy the ride.

As Officer Brimm pulled into the station, he parked on the ramp to remove Spencer and place him in the cell while he found a Detective for Spencer to talk with. As he went around to open the back door of the Police car, Officer Garcia walked by.

"What's up Artie? Where the hell have you been?" Officer Brimm asked.

"Hey bro, I took a few days off, had to take care of some personal shit. What you got, you need help?" Artie asked. "Yeah, can you take him in and put him in a cell, I need to find a Detective for this guy, he says he did something, but I told him to hold up. I read him his rights cause he was crying and talking shit in between so just in case, I read them. But just put him in the cell for me, I'll be right back," Officer Brimm advised as he motioned towards the prisoner processing area.

Artie nodded and responded, "Got you, bro." Artie bent down to remove the male from the back seat. Spencer opened his eyes, and Artie pulled him out of the car. "What the fuck are you doing in the back seat cuffed Spencer? What are you doing, what is going on?" Artie demanded.

Spencer began to sob again and told Artie what happened. Spencer continued rambling with tears flowing down his face. He told Artie that he couldn't live with the secret anymore. Artie told him that he could lose his job if he said anything about him. "Why didn't you call me baby?" Artie asked, his demeanor softening.

"I couldn't find my phone, I just couldn't get myself together!" Spencer replied staring down at his hands as Artie uncuffed him. As the lovers were talking with each other, Officer Brimm walked up and looked at Artie with his eyes opened wide and asked, "you know him, bro?"

Officer Eric Brimm startled Garcia when he asked him if he knew Spencer. "Yo bro, did you call him baby? What the fuck is going on dude?" Brimm asked.

"No man, I don't know him. He was telling me about his baby, that this is why he's all fucked up today!" Artie responded. "Anyway, I'll take over if you want, I'll babysit until Detective Lewis comes down," Artie added.

Officer Brimm smiled his appreciation to Garcia, "thanks man, I have to go meet this chick downtown at Starbucks, I met her online, but just in case she doesn't match her picture, I can always tell her I have an emergency. She won't know I'm off duty," Officer Brimm said laughing. "Thanks, man!" he added.

Garcia waved him off, "Yeah, no problem, just know that you owe me, I hope she looks like a horse," Artie teased Eric as he walked Spencer into the processing room.

Spencer looked at Artie with disgust. "You don't know me? What the fuck do you mean you don't know me?" Spencer sat down still handcuffed and pretended that he was alone.

He sat and waited patiently for Detective Lewis to come to interview him. Artie tried to plead with Spencer to let him know that if he told the Detective any information involving him, he could get suspended and possibly fired for covering up evidence that involved a murder.

Artie frowned his face and turned to Spencer, "What happened to you, why are you acting out today, what triggered this today, don't you know that I love you, you are my heart!" Artie pleaded.

"No, you don't know me, REMEMBER?" Spencer reminded Artie of his conversation with Officer Eric Brimm.

"Hey Garcia, what's going on bro? Is this the guy who has information for me?" asked Detective Lewis. Artie cleared his throat and tried to act natural, "Hey Lewis, yeah, this is the guy that Brimm picked up, but I'm not sure what the entire story is, which is why he is here. Brimm told me to tell you that he read the gentleman his rights because he was in the back seat uttering different things." Artie advised as Detective Lewis nodded.

"Ok, I'll take him from here. I'll talk to him in Room two," Lewis said. "I'll stay here with you," Garcia said. "Nah, I got it. I like to give them their privacy, you know how I roll," Lewis said.

"So tell me, sir, what's your name, and why are you here? I'm going to record our conversation so speak as clearly as you can, ok? Do you want any water or coffee?" Detective Lewis asked.

Spencer didn't respond to the question. He just began to speak from his heart, "Mmmm…my name is Spencer, Spencer McIntyre, and I think I may have killed someone!" Detective Lewis looked up from her pad, and stared directly into Spencer's sad, wet hazel eyes and asked, "What did you just say?"

Chapter 32

Randy Jr. sat on the edge of his bunk bed with his head in his hands as he read the letter from Raine. She was eager for them to exchange wedding vows once Randy Jr. was released from prison. Raine wrote Randy Jr. loving poems when they were apart.

Raine was head over heels in love with Randy Jr. which he used to his advantage. He had Raine transporting Percocet, Vicodin, and methamphetamine for him. His boy Reggie met with Raine every Monday before her shift.

Reggie packed Raine's Gucci Duffle bag with enough pills and meth to keep the entire prison high for a few days. Randy Jr. earned more money hustling inside the prison than he could have ever received on the streets.

The prison had more people, packed into a small space. That translated to more customers for Randy Jr. He even had staff members and guards hooked on his products. Randy Jr. was the man.

He received special privileges from the other guards. He had his own cell to himself and also kept a cell phone on him at all times so he could communicate with his boy, Reggie.

Although he tried not to think about her, Randy Jr. missed his mother. He wanted to call her, but he knew that if he heard her voice, it would break him. Florence and Randy Jr. had a special bond between them.

It broke him inside when his mother cried at his sentencing hearing the last time. She begged him to never leave her again. Randy Jr. couldn't do anything to help his mother. Randy Jr. knew when he promised her that he would stay out of trouble, that he wouldn't be able to keep that promise.

Randy Jr. was addicted.

The fast money, the loose women and the drug game were addicting. There was an allure that he couldn't fight. Since he was little, Randy Jr. was determined to take care of his family. Watching his mother and father work and struggle to provide for them for years was too much for him to bear.

He loved his mother so much, but he couldn't give her enough money to live and survive off of if he lived the ordinary life. The drug game provided for his mother, Sidney and his brother Cero. They didn't know it, but the game was the reason why the lights remained on and why Sidney had gas money to go home every other weekend when she was in the academy.

Randy Jr. made sure that his mother had more than enough money. Even though he couldn't sit on the phone and explain to his mother how much he loved her, Randy Jr. mailed her a check every month like clockwork. That was his best option at the moment.

Randy Jr. replayed the words that his attorney spoke earlier that day in his head. "I'm working on getting your case tossed out," he confessed as Randy Jr. stared at him blankly. Randy Jr. was happy to hear that there was a chance for him to be released, but he didn't get his hopes up.

Plenty of hard knocks taught Randy Jr. that he couldn't trust anyone. He couldn't take anyone at their word. Randy Jr. only believed action.

He thanked his attorney and walked out of the meeting area without showing emotion, but he felt plenty. Randy Jr. felt heavy emotions as he walked towards his cell. He silently prayed that God would have mercy on him and help him get released.

While he was guilty of plenty of crimes, he knew that he didn't kill Sunshine. Randy Jr. was pissed that he didn't get a chance to shoot the Bitch for stealing from him but he didn't get to her in time. By the time Randy Jr. caught up with Sunshine, she was already dead.

Someone had slit her throat from ear to ear. He wasn't too shattered over her death. Sunshine deserved everything she got. Randy Jr. was sure that she robbed the wrong person and they ended her life for it.

Randy Jr. received news that should have had him jumping for joy, but all he could do was put his head in his hands in despair. True, his attorney was working on getting him out of prison, but he had an issue much more significant than his prison sentence.

He stared at the sonogram image in complete shock. Randy Jr. went nearly 26 years without having any children. Now that he was locked in prison for life, both of his girls were pregnant.

Ciera was already four months pregnant and according to the picture he held in his hands, so was Raine. Randy Jr. was about to be a father times two. He had to find a way out of the mess he got himself into. More importantly, he needed to recruit more runners before both of his women went out on maternity leave.

As Savannah walked past his open cell door, Randy Jr. whistled to her. Savannah stopped in her tracks and turned to face Randy Jr. Savannah was a tall, thin woman with a Caesar haircut. She had a pretty face, but her body wasn't hot at all. Randy Jr. wouldn't have ordinarily wasted his time with Savannah, but based on the news Raine dropped on him, he needed a new body on his team.

Savanna leaned forward before she spoke, giving Randy Jr. a full view of her tiny breasts. He wasn't impressed but pretended to be. "Hey Gorgeous, I was thinking about you all last night," he said as she blushed sheepishly.

Randy Jr. almost laughed at how easy it was. He had another one wrapped around his finger.

Chapter 33

Garcia ran along the track, pumping his fists and legs as he tried to gain momentum. He was on a mission to clear his mind. Garcia had so many things to think about.

He thought about Sidney. She was on his mind day and night. Weeks had passed since he gave her the folder. He didn't understand why it was taking her so long to let Mystic go. Garcia expected Sidney to turn Mystic in by now. It burned him up inside when he thought about Mystic walking free, living like a King. He was tired of Mystic being the one to get the girl.

He was tired of Mystic, period. Garcia was ready to see Mystic face the consequences of his actions, for once. For years, Garcia and Mystic both competed for the affection of Sidney Stevens.

It destroyed him to know that Mystic gained Sidney's affection and trust. Garcia knew that Mystic wasn't the beacon of integrity that everyone made him out to be. He knew about Mystic's secrets, and all of the skeletons hidden in his closet.

He was just waiting on the proper time to drop a dime. That is what Garcia was good at doing, dropping dimes.

Garcia was tired of being overlooked for promotions and ignored when accolades were given out. He was tired of watching people who didn't work as hard as he did, earn more.

Garcia was ready to make a change. He was prepared to be the person who received accolades. He was ready to swear on the Bible and be ranked higher than his current position. Since they were in the Academy together, Mystic had to have the best of everything.

When Garcia set his sights on Sidney, he told Mystic. He introduced Mystic to Sidney. Garcia thought that Mystic would help fast track Sidney into the job that she was vying for. He didn't expect Mystic to steal the girl of his dreams.

He wanted Sidney all to himself.

Garcia continued running as the sun beat down on his glistening skin. He thought about Sidney. He just knew that when he showed Sidney the Police report, she would be head over heels for him. He at least expected a kiss, but Sidney shoved the folder in her bag and left the restaurant like it was nothing.

Garcia followed Sidney after she left the restaurant that evening. He knew that she was going straight to Mystic and just as expected, Sidney went directly to him. It pained Garcia that Sidney was still interested in Mystic. He was a chump.

Garcia knew exactly what he had to do to get Mystic out of the way. He had a plan. He devised the plan the day of Mystic's confirmation ceremony. Soon everyone would face their justice.

To make things happen, Garcia had to keep his hands clean. He shook his head in sadness as he slowed down his running pace. What he had to do next would be a significant step in his life.

He pulled his cell phone out of the pocket of his running shorts and opened his inbox. The last viewed message was still open. There was no text, only a picture. The image seared Garcia's brain. It was an image of Spencer on his knees with his eyes closed and Garcia deep in his throat. The image was excellent, showing both of their faces, clearly.

This wasn't the first message that Garcia received. Steven had been harassing him with pictures and threats to reveal his sexual identity. In exchange for his silence, Steven wanted Garcia to do something that made Garcia's stomach sink. He hated the very thought of what Steven instructed of him, but he couldn't imagine the backlash that he would receive if he were outed as a homosexual male.

The guys on the force would turn their backs on him for good. There would be no returning from a situation such as that. Garcia was willing to do anything to protect his image.

Steven had enough receipts and information on Garcia that he wouldn't be able to deny any of the accusations. Garcia made a decision to throw caution to the wind and follow through with his mission.

"There's no turning back from here," Garcia said as he made up his mind about what he wanted to do, next.

Chapter 34

Vondra cried as she climbed on the hard mattress in her prison cell. She couldn't get over the situation she found herself in. Everything seemed unreal to her. One minute she was sleeping on her couch with her child by her side and the next she was being dragged out of her house by the Police.

Everyone kept telling her that her name was something completely different. She felt like she was losing her mind.

Vondra couldn't make sense of any of it. She heard the guard's footsteps growing closer, and she began to cringe inside. She wished that she could disappear into a tiny ball.

"Vondra, the doctor, is here to see you," the guard called as he waited for a response from her. She didn't move. She could hear the doctor's footsteps approaching, but she didn't turn to face him. "Mrs. Mystic, I am Dr. Krysinski. I am here to evaluate you," he said as Vondra curled her body up tighter into a ball.

"Vondra, you were last seen at the Psychological Services Center is that correct?" he asked as she shook her head furiously. "Is your doctor, Sidney Stevens?" she asked as Vondra began to shake her head vigorously.

"NO!" she screamed as he continued to speak. "We have arranged to return you back to the North Florida Mental Hospital facility under their 24-hour program," he advised, "so that we can get you evaluated to see if you are fit to stand trial. You are aware of your charges correct? But first we have to give you something to help you relax for the ride," he explained.

"NOOO!" Vondra screamed as the guard held her body down and allowed the doctor to insert the syringe needle in her vein. "I'm not Vondra!" she screamed as the doctor continued to insert the liquid into her vein.

Instantly, Vondra's mood changed. She no longer fought against the restraints. She just laid there on the bed staring at the ceiling. Vondra listened as the doctors talked about transferring her from Texas to the Medical Center in Florida. Vondra wanted to tell them that they had it all wrong, but she couldn't.

She could only cry.

Vondra laid in bed as she awaited her transfer. Three hours after her medication was administered, Vondra was transferred to the prison van. She didn't realize that she was being moved, however. The Thorazine in her system kept her lulled into a comfortable sleep.

Vondra slept the entire ride to the North Florida Mental Hospital. When she opened her eyes, they were pulling into the driveway of the hospital. Vondra's eyes widened as she was taken in the facility.

The medication that she was administered must have been strong because she was still unable to stand on her own. When the guard opened the back door of the van, she merely smiled at him.

Her guard rolled his eyes as he tapped his finger impatiently on the top of his gun. He was ready to use lethal force on Vondra. Vondra's eyes bore into the prison guard's dark brown eyes, and she saw something sinister in them.

He wanted to use the gun on her, especially with her history, but Vondra refused to give him a reason, however.

The guard roughly grabbed Vondra's arm and sat her in the wheelchair. The other guard stood in front of Vondra holding his service weapon in front of her, cautiously. Vondra smirked at the guard.

She wondered why they were on edge. "Alright Vondra, it's time for you to go back to your home," the guard said with an empathetic smile as Vondra rolled her eyes at him. "I am not Vondra!" she yelled as the guard wheeled her inside the hospital.

Vondra took in the sights of the hospital. Everything seemed so new. Her eyes darted from one side of the hospital to the other as she assessed the inside of the facility.

The guard wheeled her to the front desk and spoke to the charge nurse. "Good morning Ms. Christianson. I need to check Vondra Mystic into the hospital. I have her papers from the courts with me and her diagnosis from her prior physician," he said.

Vera stood in front of the desk in complete shock. She dropped the phone that was in her hand and walked to the opposite side of the counter to see Vondra. Vera stood in front of Vondra, she got almost close enough for their faces to touch then she jumped back in surprise. After the havoc she wreaked on the facility, the devil was back again.

Vondra stared angrily at Vera. "Hello!" she said as Vera shook her head sadly at the pitiful sight in front of her. Although Vera was happy to have Vondra back, she couldn't shake the strange feeling she had. Vera stared at Vondra as she swung her long hair over her shoulder, noting that something was different about her.

"Welcome back. I'm sure you remember the rules here. Play nice, Vondra," Vera warned as she noticed the grimace growing on Vondra's face.

Chapter 35

Randy Jr. kept in constant contact with Sidney. She begged Randy Jr. to talk to their mother about his situation. Sidney assumed that he said something to his mother because Florence stopped asking about Randy Jr. and only said prayers for him.

Florence was a smart woman. She knew when her son was up to no good or in trouble.

Suddenly, Sidney's cell phone began to vibrate. She glanced down at the number, and her heartbeat quickened. Sidney wanted to answer the phone but was afraid of what she might hear.

Instead, she closed her eyes and tried to calm her nerves.

When she was finally able to compose herself, Sidney redialed the phone number. Randy Jr. answered on the first ring. "What's up, sis?" he asked as Sidney laughed. "Only you could get access to a phone in prison. What's up?" she asked.

"Sid, that Billingsley guy helped me set up an account for you to use," he announced proudly. "I'm going to have the bank card mailed to you," he said.

Sidney was happy to hear from her brother. It also helped that he had extra money for his defense attorney fees. Sidney knew that it was time to get some extra help for her mother, especially with Cero. Sidney ended the call feeling relieved.

Sidney worried about her mother and her brothers. She also worried about herself. Sidney was ready for a change. Sidney's cell phone began to vibrate, interrupting her thoughts. She glanced down at the phone, and her heart skipped a beat. "Finally!" she said as she answered the phone. "Hi, Dr. Streeter!" she said excitedly as he chuckled.

"I bet you thought I forgot about you, huh?" he teased. "Not at all. I know that you are a man of your word," she said as he laughed on the other end.

After exchanging pleasantries, Dr. Streeter's tone changed from joyful to serious as he got down to business.

"Sidney, I have some information on Marcus Mystic, and it doesn't look good. There are over two dozen brutality complaints against him. He was even brought in front of a grand jury twice when suspects in his custody ended up deceased upon arrival to the precinct," Dr. Streeter continued talking as Sidney's head spun with disgust.

The man she loved was nothing more than a monster. "Look, I can send you the case files for each, but it will take a while. Everything is sealed," Dr. Streeter explained as Sidney wiped away her tears.

Sidney reared back in her office chair and closed her eyes. She had to get herself together, but she struggled with the news Dr. Streeter just shared. Sidney considered calling Mystic but immediately thought against the idea. She didn't know what she would say to him, and Sidney was convinced he would only lie if she asked him about the brutality complaints. At least she knew the truth, now.

"Thank you for doing this for me," Sidney said sadly. Dr. Streeter could hear the tears in her voice. "Are you okay, Sidney?" he asked concerned. "Yes, I'm fine. It's just been a long day. Thank you for giving me the update," she said eagerly. Dr. Streeter sighed heavily in response. Sidney held her breath as she waited for Dr. Streeter to continue speaking.

"Sidney, I have the names of the Officers you were seeking. I also located the original Police report. I'm going to text you a picture of both," he said.

"Thank you!" Sidney squealed as he cleared his throat to interrupt her celebrating. "You must promise me that you will destroy this document and the message after you receive it," he advised.

Sidney agreed and thanked her mentor again. When she hung up the phone, she sat it directly in front of her and waited for his text message.

Ten minutes later, her cell phone vibrated with a message. Sidney opened the message and read the names. Her blood boiled as she noticed the final name listed on the Police report. Frustrated and angry, Sidney grabbed the phone and dialed Garcia's phone number.

When she didn't receive a response, Sidney stood up from her desk and grabbed her keys.

"It's time to get to the bottom of this," Sidney said as she left her office.

Chapter 36

The breeze from the ocean wafted through his office window as Mystic walked around his desk to greet the Mayor. "Mayor Sturgin, come in, your honor," he said as he shook the Mayor's hand.

"Please have a seat," he offered as his secretary walked inside and placed two cold bottles of water on the table in front of him and quickly left the office.

Mayor Bill Sturgin was a white-haired old man with old country boy values. Standing at less than five feet tall, his portly belly was the biggest thing on him. He was a stern man and very direct. Mystic loved the fact that the Mayor didn't beat around the bush.

Mystic sat down and waited for the Mayor to begin speaking. "Marcus, I'm concerned," he said as Mystic attempted to massage the tension away from his forehead. "What can I help you with, sir?" Mystic asked. Over almost two decades on the force taught Mystic how to handle situations like this. He watched as the Mayor put on a performance of sipping his water and wiping his mouth before he continued speaking.

"This town has become a mess. I promised the constituents of this city that I would clean up the streets. The stats don't look good, Marcus," he whined as he handed Mystic the crime data report.

"Look at this mess!" he said as Marcus pretended to review the figures. He didn't take the time to remind the Mayor that it was his office that provided the crime data. He knew what the statistics looked like. Mystic just wondered what the Mayor expected him to do about the recent influx of crime.

"I need something big. Something to reassure the public that I have a handle on the crime in this city," he said as Mystic considered his words. The Mayor wiped the sweat from his forehead and leaned forward. "If I can't deliver results, I can't get reelected," he said.

"If I don't get reelected....you do know your position is political right?" he teased with a wink as Mystic frowned in response. Mystic despised threats, and he knew precisely where the Mayor was heading with the conversation.

Mayor Sturgin looked around the office and smiled. "It is really nice in here Marcus. I'm sure you love driving your department issued vehicle and the perks that you have been given. I have heard strange things about this office lately," he continued as Mystic's eyes narrowed.

"Marcus, please don't let me find out that you haven't been performing your duties as Chief of Police appropriately. I was the one who recommended you for this job," he advised.

Mystic burned with the desire to tell the Mayor that he didn't ask him to run on that platform. He wasn't responsible for the crime data, but instead, he said something completely different.

He stood from his seat and walked around his office nervously. Mystic knew that once he said what he was thinking, everything in his life would change.

Mystic didn't respond, immediately. He thought about what the Mayor said and then answered slowly. "Not to worry, sir, my team is working the Killa Dre case," he said proudly as the Mayor's ears perked up.

An arrest in the Killa Dre case would be beneficial for the entire department. After a few years of corruption issues within the Police department, many in the community had lost faith. The Killa Dre murder was so gruesome even the thugs on the streets were scared.

The street thugs knew that once the top dog was killed, the second in line would step up and run the streets. After Killa Dre's murder, no one stepped up. There was no control over the drug pipeline. The streets began to erupt in violence.

Bringing Killa Dre's murderer to justice would help heal the community and put things back at ease. It also meant that the cops who were on Killa Dre's payroll and the Mayor, in particular, would feel vindicated for their financial losses.

They all took a financial hit when Killa Dre was murdered. The Mayor promised himself that he would see to it that Killa Dre's murderer sat in the electric chair for his crimes. It broke Mayor Sturgin down when he couldn't buy his wife the new Tiffany diamond ring she wanted.

All of that he blamed on Killa Dre's murderer.

If they could bring the killer in and throw the book at him, they could kill the drug pipeline to the community and help him sleep better at night. The Mayor was finally feeling better. In fact, Marcus gave him better news than he had anticipated.

"Killa Dre? Wow, that would be something amazing to add to my record. A conviction for the murder of the communities biggest drug lord. This is huge!" the Mayor said with excitement. "This would signify something big for the community. We could proclaim that the drug king was taken out and we have the next in line in our custody! Good job Marcus!" he said with a chuckle.

"I knew you were perfect for this job. I knew you wouldn't let me down. Put everyone in the department on this. I want to place all of our resources on this case. We will bring Killa Dre's killer to justice!" he said with a roar of enthusiasm.

Chapter 37

Florence held the phone in her hands and giggled loudly as the automated teller informed her of her new balance. $212, 345.00 were sitting in Florence's savings account. She currently had more money in her bank account then she had ever seen in her lifetime.

She didn't know what to do with herself.

Florence imagined all of the things that she would do with the extra money. She wanted to buy a house and move her family out of the projects. Cero deserved a better environment. She imagined Cero going to the best boarding school that money could buy. The top school for Autism.

Florence had dreams, and now that her bank account looked fuller, she was able to make her dreams come true. She had God and China Doll, Inc to thank for her good fortune. Florence didn't tell Sidney, but the checks continued to come, and they increased in value.

Thanks to a mysterious stranger, she had enough money to provide for her family and to live her dreams. Florence was happy with her life.

She just had one dilemma. She didn't know whether to share her newfound wealth with her daughter or keep it to herself. She knew that Sidney would immediately question the source of her funds. Florence recalled the way her daughter reacted when she showed her the first checks she received.

Sidney would launch a full-on investigation into the matter. Florence didn't want all of that to happen so instead, she decided to keep her money a secret.

"Momma!" Cero called out from the living room. Florence slowly made her way to her son and shook her head when she noticed the mess he made.

Cero had shredded paper all over the floor. Florence bent down to pick up the mess, and suddenly she felt a sharp pain in her chest.

She tried to sit down on the couch to catch her breath, but she suddenly dropped to the floor. Cero tapped his mother on her shoulder. "Momma?" he asked as her eyes began to close shut.

Three hours later, Florence awoke inside a sterile hospital room. She looked around and tried to make sense of her surroundings. "Mom are you okay?" Sidney asked as she jumped from her seat, next to her mother's hospital bed.

"What in the world?" Florence asked as she finally noticed the wires and IV lines connected to her. "What happened?" she questioned, while her daughter covered her face with kisses.

"Mom, you had a stroke. You've been in this hospital for a week. You just woke up from a coma!" Sidney exclaimed as her mother tried to sit up in the bed.

"Where is Cero?" Florence asked as she looked around the room searching for her son. "Mom, he's doing just fine. Mr. Earl offered to watch him.

"He's been at our house every single day since you were admitted here. Mom, I'm so glad that he found you in time. I can't imagine what would have happened if Mr. Earl didn't decide to check in on you," Sidney cried as her mother listened to her daughter speak, in shock.

"Mom, I think we need to discuss placing Cero in a special school for people with Autism," Sidney advised. "I think this is too much on you," she said. "You could have died, Mom! I can't live without you," Sidney wailed as she threw her arms around her mother.

"I called Randy Jr., and he is praying for you, Mom. He said that soon he would be able to call you," she said hopefully. She knew that Randy Jr. wouldn't call their mother until his release.

Florence pursed her lips and shot her daughter a side-eye glance.

"Girl, stop that crying. God is a healer, and I am faithful. I know that he wouldn't take me from y'all right now. Especially with your brother in that prison," she said as Sidney shot her a strange look.

She didn't expect her brother to come clean about his prison time so soon. When Sidney spoke with Randy Jr., he assured her that he would take care of everything.

She smiled with pride. At least he kept his word in that regard.

"Don't look at me like that. I know my children, and I know when they are trying to hide something from me," she said with a smile. "I might have had a stroke, but I still got my senses," Florence said proudly.

She didn't tell Sidney, but she had already enrolled Cero in the Carrie Brazer Center for Autism. Florence also withheld her biggest surprise. She amassed enough money in her account to purchase a modest home in Broward County. Florence was finally about to become a homeowner. She was proud of her family and their progress.

Although things in their life weren't exactly perfect. She was blessed to see God's hand working in her children's lives and her own. It felt good to know that finally, things were starting to work out for her.

Florence smiled and looked up at the sky, "I'm still holding on, Randy," she said as she wiped away a tear.

Chapter 38

Spencer didn't rest the entire time he remained in the jail cell. He kept his eyes on the other two male occupants inside the small living quarters with him. Spencer heard about the horror stories people told about jail and what he saw on TV. He refused to become a victim.

Luckily, the inmates remained cordial with Spencer, and no one tried any funny business with him.

He had been locked in the jail cell for nearly three weeks. His attorney assured him that he would find a way for Spencer to be released. Isaac was determined and persistent, both qualities that Spencer needed to get down to the root of his case.

His attorney promised him that he would find a way to have Spencer released on a bond soon. Spencer prayed that the judge would have pity on him and offer at least a $100,000 bond. Spencer's record was clean, he never committed a crime in his life aside from the occasional bounced check.

Spencer knew that soon he would be out of the jail. That is how he maintained his composure throughout the problematic days within the industrial complex.

He forced himself to eat his food without gagging. No matter how terrible the food looked, he forced it down. The sloppy joes contained unidentified meat crumbles, and the food was always bland and cold. The vegetables were undercooked, and there was never any good dessert left, but Spencer didn't complain.

Spencer spent his free time writing to his family and his friends. Sidney wrote to him once, telling him how much she supported him and believed in his innocence. Spencer read and re-read letters to keep himself encouraged.

He exercised inside his cell to maintain his fitness. Outside of jail, Spencer was a homosexual male, but inside the jail, he was just Spencer.

Spencer made sure that he behaved in the manner that was expected of a manly man. He employed his acting skills while in jail. Spencer didn't converse with anyone, and he rarely shared emotion. Spencer did everything that he could do to avoid attention.

When he was allowed phone time, he dialed Artie's number religiously. He called Artie daily. He dialed Artie's number more than he dialed his own mother's phone number.

At first, he figured that Artie was busy and out on the beat. After the twentieth missed call, Spencer thought that Artie didn't want to get involved in the murder case. Spencer stopped calling Artie when he left messages that were never returned.

It broke his heart to see how Artie treated him after they shared so much love with each other. He couldn't believe that Artie kicked him to the curb over a false murder charge.

Spencer figured that Artie's comrades finally persuaded him to let go. Spencer was convinced in his heart that Artie wouldn't voluntarily turn his back on him. Either way, he didn't bother worrying about Artie or anyone who didn't call him. Spencer didn't want to fall into the despair of depression.

Worrying about Artie would surely drive him there.

Spencer watched the soap opera in the dayroom on the one television they had. He tried to get into it, but he hated daytime television. He really didn't have a choice in a shared environment with over 150 men inside.

He finally started to get into the show when he heard the guards approaching. Uncomfortable with someone walking up behind him, Spencer turned around quickly and faced the guard. "Your lawyer is here to see you," the guard announced as he walked Spencer to the private visiting lounge. He smiled at his attorney and sat down in front of him.

"So, what do you have for me?" Spencer asked with hopefulness in his voice. Isaac let out a slow breath and folded his hands. "Well, Spencer I have to be honest with you. It doesn't look too good for you right now," he said sadly.

Isaac reached inside his briefcase and retrieved a folder. He slid the folder across the table and waited for Spencer to open it. When Spencer opened the folder, he gasped in fright. Sitting on top of a thick stack of papers was a picture.

It was a photograph of Linda's mouth. Spencer began hyperventilating as he stared at the image. "Oh, my God!" Spencer said as his attorney stared at him expectantly.

"Spencer have you seen this before?" he asked as Spencer nodded with tears flowing freely down his cheeks. For the first time since his ordeal began, Spencer cried. He wept loudly as Isaac called his name softly. "Spencer... are you ok?" he asked.

"How...How did you get this?" Spencer stammered as the attorney shrugged. "It was entered into evidence several days ago by an Officer A. Garcia," Isaac responded as Spencer gasped.

Artie turned in the package that Steven delivered! Why would Artie turn in the package? Spencer wondered about Artie's plan. He figured somehow, some way Artie was doing it to save him.

That's when it all hit him. Steven may have done it. What if Steven was trying to frame him by intimidating Artie. "Oh, God you have to help him. Steven may be trying to kill Artie! Artie is in danger!" he yelled as the attorney raised his hands to calm Spencer.

"Spencer, I don't think you understand. Officer Arturo Garcia is the person who turned you in. Here is his statement," he said passing Spencer the photocopied document.

Spencer wept loudly as he read Artie's acidic words; the very words that put him in the hell he currently resided.

Chapter 39

Randy Jr. placed the money in his pocket and kicked his feet around in the grass. He was outside enjoying the hour of recreation time or at least that's what he wanted the guards to believe. Randy Jr. was really in the middle of a drug sale.

He sold the last of his product that afternoon. He couldn't wait for his girl Raine to come in later that evening. She was carrying the re-up for his next sale. He had depleted all of his stashes. The prisoners were hooked on his product, and he was hooked on the money that came in. The money was fast, and Randy Jr. used it to control the prison.

In less than a year, Randy Jr. had amassed a fortune in the prison. He stashed his money in an account that he established for his sister. Randy Jr. glanced at his cell phone and smiled broadly. The money he sent with his girl, Ciera had already been deposited. "Good girl," Randy Jr. said closing out the application. He trusted Ciera with his money. She could make a deposit without Reggie's involvement.

Randy Jr. preferred to keep his accounts separate. He alternated between Ciera and Reggie for deposits. This kept everyone honest. Randy Jr. didn't believe in letting his right hand know what the left hand was doing.

He never forgot that most gangsters were brought down by the people closest to them. Randy Jr. didn't believe in keeping anyone too close.

Reggie had his back, however. He made sure that everything operated smoothly with his business. Randy Jr. heard the whistle and began walking towards the gate to wait for the guards.

When he entered the prison walls, his guard tapped his shoulder. "Mr. Billingsley is here to see you," he whispered as Randy Jr. nodded. He screened his visitors better than a CEO.

The minute Randy Jr. opened the door and saw Mr. Billingsley seated at the table he beamed with excitement. Mr. Billingsley didn't wait for him to sit down, he jumped up from his seat and embraced Randy Jr. Randy Jr. pushed him back and looked around to see if anyone witnessed the hug.

When he was assured that no one was watching he turned and faced the attorney. "What the fuck was that all about?" he asked with a frustrated frown.

Mr. Billingsley blushed and began to sweat. "I apologize. I was just excited. You're getting out of here!" he announced as Randy Jr. smiled. "It's about time," he said with a grin.

"How did you make that happen?" Randy Jr. asked as he sat down and shot Mr. Billingsley a curious look. "Well, it turns out that Sunshine was murdered by her pimp. He is a well-known criminal who has confessed to the murder," he said as Randy Jr. sat there stunned and surprised.

After a few minutes, he finally spoke, "So how long before you get me out of here?" he asked. Mr. Billingsley smiled even broader. "I can have you out of here by tomorrow," he said excitedly.

Randy Jr. thought about the predicament he was in. Two of the guards were carrying his babies. He had amassed a fortune in prison and had gained many customers. He considered what Mr. Billingsley said and nodded. "I'll be waiting," he said with a chuckle.

Chapter 40

Mystic drove towards the projects with a plan in mind. Three full-time crews worked the Killa Dre murder case and sadly he didn't see the case moving at all. Mystic didn't want to turn Randy Jr. in but he realized that if he didn't, he would soon be on the chopping block.

He considered his next move carefully. He had to do something, quick.

Aunt Vera called him incessantly. She left him messages to contact her, but he didn't return her calls. Vondra wasn't a top priority for him. Mystic knew that his wife wouldn't try to harm him. She would hurt everyone else, but she wouldn't touch him.

He didn't have the capacity to think about Vondra. His mind was on Sidney. He thought about her every day. The last time he saw her was when he kissed her. She refused to talk to him again, and it made him uneasy. Mystic wondered if Sidney found out more information about him.

He racked his brain trying to identify who shared the Police report with Sidney.

He couldn't even lie if she showed him the report. Mystic would be forced to tell her the truth. He would have to tell her that he was there that night that her father was killed. He would confess to being there after lying to her about it for weeks.

Sidney would never trust him again.

Mystic feared that after all the effort it took to gain Sidney's trust, he would destroy it all with a lie. He had to find a way to make it alright again. He would lay in bed all night trying to find a way out of his mess. The sleep deprivation, coupled with a lack of nutrition was sending Mystic's brain into haywire.

Mystic was losing his mind.

He decided that once he got rid of Killa Dre's hand, he would take a long vacation. He needed to get away from the Police Department, and he also needed to put some physical distance between him and Sidney.

Mystic considered moving away to another state. He figured that would be a viable way to start completely over. He pulled his Tahoe over to the side of the road and parked. He opened the door and looked around to make sure that no one was following behind him.

It was dark outside so he figured that no one would be out in the secluded area. He just wanted to bury the hand and get away. Mystic surmised that in a few weeks he would send his Detectives out to where he currently was, and claim that someone called in a tip to their crime hotline.

Although it was dark outside, Mystic was sure to be extra careful. He took his time and ambled quietly, carrying a small shovel to a wooded area. He reached inside of a black garbage bag and retrieved the sack with the hand safely inside.

Mystic began to dig when he heard a noise. He turned around to investigate the strange sound and faced bright lights. He shielded his eyes from the rays, hoping that the culprit would turn them off. "Turn off your lights!" Mystic finally yelled when the person shined the flashlight in his face.

"Identify yourself!" the person yelled as Mystic covered his face. He had to get away from the flashlight-wielding person. Mystic's entire career and life would go up in flames if he were identified outside, trespassing with evidence from a murder in his possession.

"I had to piss" he explained. "Be out of your way in a sec," he said shielding his eyes from the blinding lights.

"Chief? Is that you?" he heard in the distance. Mystic had to think fast. His instinct told him to run, but he couldn't move. He turned to run, but a heavy hand fell on his shoulder.

"Chief, we received a tip that someone was out here on the highway, acting suspicious, carrying a shovel and large garbage bag," the officer said shining the light on Mystic. "Well, now that you know that it's me, turn off the damn light!" Mystic instructed angrily. The officer ignored his statement and moved the flashlight towards Mystic's hands.

When the flashlight hit the plastic bag and the shovel he stared at Mystic with a question in his eyes. "What do you have there?" he asked reaching for the bag. When he opened the bag and noticed the hand, he jumped and dropped the bag on the ground.

Mystic turned to run but was apprehended by another officer who slapped handcuffs on his wrists. "Chief Marcus Mystic, you are being detained and transported for questioning of possession of evidence involving the murder of Andre Stewart, AKA Killa Dre," he said as he walked Mystic to the awaiting police vehicle.

"No!" Mystic screamed. "You have the wrong guy!" he yelled as the Officers placed him inside the back of the police car. They towed Mystic's Tahoe to the station for further investigation.

Chapter 41

Garcia gripped the newspaper in his hands as he sipped his coffee at the bay window overlooking the ocean. The paper boasted a picture of Chief Marcus Mystic splashed across the front page with a startling headline. The headline read, "Corrupted Chief!"

Garcia tried not to laugh when he saw the look of surprise on Mystic's face. After years of hard work, he was finally being recognized for his service and dedication to the department. The FBI had been investigating Mystic for several months, and with Garcia's help, they were finally able to bring him down. Garcia felt vindicated. He was promised an excellent, cushy job in the Bureau after graduation from the FBI Academy.

Nine months ago, Garcia was approached by the head of the Florida Field Office about rampant Police misconduct. Garcia initially refused the case. He was too loyal to the department and his brothers on the force to betray any of them. Then, Ken Mursty showed Garcia a picture of their target. When Garcia saw the smug look on Mystic's face in the photo Ken was holding, he couldn't help himself. He had to join the investigation. The day he decided to become an FBI informant, Garcia applied to the FBI Academy.

It was all too perfect for him not to.

Garcia wanted to bury Mystic, and now he had the chance. His superiors were well aware of Mystic's criminal activity and Police brutality issues, but they brushed it all under the rug. Garcia had to work overtime to get the necessary dirt on Mystic.

As images of Vivica, the receptionist in the Police Records Department flashed through his mind, he shuddered in disgust. Once he got over the sheer repugnance of seeing Vivica naked, Garcia had no problem acquiring access to every file he needed on Mystic.

Vivica wasn't a horrible looking woman, but Garcia was a picky man. Still, he pleased Vivica enough to make her putty in his hands.

Although he would never admit to it, Garcia envisioned himself making love to Sidney while he caressed Vivica's body. She moaned and squealed with delight as he put his magic on her. The darkness in the bedroom helped, tremendously.

He didn't care about fucking Vivica. Garcia was aware of his appeal to both men and women alike. He wielded that power to get everything that he wanted. Garcia knew that the information he submitted to the FBI would secure a beautiful future.

Garcia also knew that with Mystic locked away, he could make his move on who he really wanted, and that was Sidney.

As the FBI's informant, Garcia supplied them with more than enough details about Mystic's criminal activity to send everyone in a frenzy.

Garcia enjoyed watching the news and reading the newspapers. Pictures of Mystic's solemn looking face made him giddy. After he supplied the FBI with their information, he waited for them to make a move on Mystic. He could see that Sidney's heart was softening towards Mystic.

He couldn't wait on the FBI any longer.

Garcia drove across town and used a burner phone to make the call to the Police Tip Line. He didn't want to be caught calling in a tip against the Chief of Police. After the tip was placed, he just sat back and watched Mystic's life unravel. It was a lovely sight. Mystic's arrest prompted the Internal Affairs department to launch an investigation of their own.

They determined that Mystic used Department funds to commit his wife to a mental hospital in northern Florida. The department covered his trips out of state and hotel stays that were not approved. The Internal Affairs Department presented a scathing investigation that found Mystic liable for embezzlement, corruption and impeding a police investigation.

Mystic's rap sheet was so long that everyone inside the courtroom sat in shocked fascination as they heard the prosecutors lay out their case against him.

It was like watching a television show. Garcia was addicted.

Garcia couldn't wait until the end of the court session that day. He would surprise Sidney with the great news.

Garcia received his acceptance letter to the FBI Academy. He was headed to Quantico. In his mind, he envisioned Sidney being so excited about the news that she throws her arms around him and they share a deep kiss. His erection throbbed against his leg as he thought about Sidney's soft body.

While they sat in court watching Mystic on the stand, Garcia couldn't help himself. He grabbed Sidney's hand and caressed it. Mystic glared at them, his eyes never leaving Garcia's. Amused by Mystic's reaction, Garcia kissed Sidney's hand gently as she leaned closer to him, Garcia never losing eye contact with Mystic.

Garcia winked at Mystic. While the simple gesture was missed by everyone else, Mystic's eyes narrowed in recognition. He saw Garcia's wink as a way of conveying to his friend that he was Sidney's protector, now.

Garcia made sure that he attended each court session. He was present when they convicted Mystic of corruption and murder. It took everything in him not to jump for joy when Mystic was slapped with 25 years in federal prison. Sidney sat beside Garcia, emotionless, throughout the trial. Garcia was thrilled to have Sidney by his side.

Garcia held Sidney's hand and consoled her when Mystic received his sentence for his participation in the murder of Killa Dre. He squeezed her hand and reiterated his feelings to her. "Sidney, don't worry. I will protect you. I am always here for you," he reminded her as she hugged him tightly.

Mystic turned and faced Garcia. He smiled and even returned a wink at Garcia and mouthed, "I'll be in touch!" as they walked him out of the courtroom. Sidney stood in the back of the courtroom and took every gesture in. Mystic knew that Garcia had something to do with his arrest and ultimate conviction. Mystic was completely innocent, but he knew that there was no way of proving it. He would take a bullet for Sidney, and keeping his silence and accepting this punishment on the Killa Dre murder was like a shot to the heart for him. The world wanted to see his head on a stake.

They were using Mystic as the poster child for Police corruption and abuse of power. His case was plastered on every news channel. The court proceedings for Chief Marcus Mystic played out on live television, just as it did in Officer Arturo Garcia's head.

It was the most watched program for the week. Mystic felt like he was owed money from the owners of the major networks for the boost in ratings, but that was a minor issue.

Garcia had one last nail to pound into the coffin. He turned over every letter that was sent to Spencer from Steven King, linking him to the murder of his wife Linda King.

Steven was picked up from an issued warrant and arrested at his home. He was charged with one count of first degree murder and threats against a Law Enforcement Officer. Garcia threw Spencer a bone and added a stalking charge as well.

Chapter 42

Sidney listened to the radio as she worked through the stacks of files on her desk. She had to do something to take her mind off of Spencer. Sidney planned to visit him at the prison after she left her office that day. Sorting through the files helped her keep her mind off the deep feeling of fear that she felt for Spencer and the pain she felt with the Mystic ordeal.

Spencer was facing a life sentence in prison for murder. Sidney knew that her friend didn't do it. She just didn't know how to help him. Instead, she threw herself into her work.

She was really starting to get the hang of her profiling position and was beginning to make great strides. Her supervisors had her looking at cases that were decades old because of her eagle eye.

Sidney could review things and pick out the most intricate detail; things that a seasoned agent may have overlooked. Sidney appreciated the respect that she was beginning to earn in her position.

As she flipped through the stack of folders that Kimberly left in her inbox, Sidney's eyes fell on a particular folder marked, Mystic. Knowing that the name,

Mystic wasn't typical, she snatched the folder from the pile and opened it.

Sidney began to read as her eyes misted with tears of regret. Marcus J. Mystic's dirty deeds were on full display. As if the details from Mystic's trial weren't heart wrenching enough, the file she read tore his credibility to shreds.

Mystic was being investigated by the FBI and the Police department. She scanned over the information concerning the investigation and gasped in shock when she saw the name listed on the notes, Arturo Vega Garcia. Garcia was listed as an FBI Informant in Mystic's case. Sidney felt a sharp pain of sadness pierce through her heart.

Tears welled up in her eyes. Sidney realized that she couldn't trust either of the men she cared about. The epiphany hurt more than any pain she felt before. Garcia wasn't who she thought he was.

She looked up when she heard a knock on her door. "Hey, Sidney. Check out this case that just came across my desk. Turns out we have another serial killer on our hands. Look at it and let me know what you think," Agent Rosstein asked as he handed Sidney the file.

Sidney thanked Agent Rosstein for the file and immediately opened it for review. The top of the file read North Florida Mental Hospital which intrigued Sidney. She continued reading, and her eyes began to widen. Vondra Duncan Mystic, Black Female, age 37 an inpatient at North Florida Mental Hospital, admitted by her husband. Sidney's eyes narrowed as she continued to read the documentation.

According to the files, Vondra murdered five people at different hospitals, including several patients. Sidney covered her mouth in surprise. "This lady is crazy!" she said as she continued to read. Sidney couldn't believe that Vondra was actually a murderer. She thought that she was crazy, but to actually kill someone was on a whole different level.

Sidney read the Docket information on Vondra in complete shock. According to the documentation, Vondra and her twin sister Elsa were both abused by their parents as children. The little girls devised a plan together to enact an act of justifiable revenge against their parents.

After their father was sentenced to prison and their mother's untimely death the girls were sent to live in a foster home. The Covingtons were loving people who treated the girls well. They understood that the girls needed help, but not to the extent that they required it.

It didn't take long for the foster family to realize that something wasn't right with Elsa and Vondra. They would often shut down communication, going completely mute for weeks on end. They were enthralled with death.

Neighbors began to complain about missing pets, and small animals were found buried on their family's property. Their foster parents didn't want to believe that the two adorable little girls with the long ponytails could harm anyone. Andrea and Ken Covington decided to have the girls evaluated for mental illness.

According to the evaluators, Vondra and Elsa were quite intelligent. They were diagnosed with many conditions including selective mutism. They would pick and choose when they wanted to converse with others. Their IQ scores were so high that they landed the girls in the "gifted" category. The only trouble, the girls, couldn't stop being violent with each other.

The twin sisters fought incessantly, but couldn't stay away from each other. They played games with unsuspecting folks by switching identities. Vondra and her sister visited several psychiatrists and therapists under their foster parent's care. It seemed like they were recovering well from their childhood trauma. Then one day a jogger found the bodies of both Andrea and Ken Covington.

Their throats had been slit.

The Police spoke with the girls through the assistance of child therapists. They switched their identities so often, no one could tell them apart.

The girls often used their likeness to their advantage. Sidney couldn't put the notes down. She never heard back from Vondra's past therapist, but she didn't need to. The information she had on her desk gave her all she needed to know about Vondra Mystic.

Sidney's mind immediately flashed back to that fateful evening inside her office. Vondra could have easily killed Sidney that day. Or was it Elsa? She didn't realize the depth of their evilness. It made her body tremble with fear. The more she thought about them, the more her mind drifted to Mystic. He claimed to love her, but all he did was unleash a fury of hurt and pain on her.

Vondra was the last straw.

Sidney took notes of the information she read. She still had to present her findings to the department supervisor. Her hands began to shake uncontrollably as she continued to learn about Vondra's psychotic acts, which as she thought back on it, it could have been Elsa.

Then she read the words that literally made her heart stop, "In the early morning hours of July 15th, Vondra Duncan Mystic escaped from the North Florida Mental Hospital. She eluded Police but was found in Texas and extradited back to North Florida where she will be evaluated and charged with the murders of three (3) individuals there, and then brought down to South Florida where she will be charged with the murder of two (2) individuals there. We are searching for more victims she may have encountered along her path. We are asking that anyone with information contact the FBI as soon as possible, you can remain anonymous.

Sidney glared at the photo, and then she took another, long look. She couldn't get over Vondra's face. Such a sadistic Booking photo. Something was off.

Sidney could only imagine the condition Vondra was in at that time. She looked at the booking photo once again, and thought to herself, "This could be either one of them!" Sidney's comfort level suddenly plummeted.

Epilogue

I mages flooded her mind as she pressed her foot on the gas pedal causing the car to accelerate. She drove along the highway considering all of the things that she endured throughout her life to bring her to this point.

It felt good to finally be free from it all. Vondra was proud of herself. She outsmarted everyone and still came out on top. That was Vondra's power. She had nine lives and a brilliant mind.

She laughed hysterically as she considered the look on her sister's face when she showed up at her house. Elsa looked like she was ready to shit a brick when Vondra stood over her. "Good for her ass!" Vondra said aloud. Her sister deserved to die for the crimes that she committed against Vondra.

They made a deal, and Elsa went back on the deal. She was supposed to give her the baby and disappear from their lives. Instead, Elsa betrayed her after all she did for her sister. Elsa deserved everything that was coming her way. Her sister was finally in the place where she belonged.

As the music played on the speakers, she hummed along to the tune. "Running back to you," Vondra sang as she imagined her husband's handsome face. After all that she had been through, she was making her way back to her husband. Vondra had no idea the downfall that Mystic had taken.

Vondra imagined the look on Mystic's face when he finally saw her. He would welcome her home with open arms once he saw who she had with her.

She turned to face the handsome little boy in the back seat, "you alright back there Marcus?" she asked as he responded with a giggle. "Yes, Ma'am."

Vondra pulled on the cigarette and exhaled a cloud of smoke. She drove down I 95 with a newfound intensity in her heart. She was heading to see the love of her life. Vondra couldn't wait to reunite her family.

Spencer MacIntyre was released from jail and all charges were dropped against him when they arrested and booked Steven King. Steven gave a full confession, after a private visit from Officer Garcia before he left for the FBI Academy. Steven did write to Spencer on three different occasions but the letters were sent back, unopened.

Spencer has since gone back to the 24 hour Gym on Miami Beach where he remains the manager.

About the Author

Frederica Paremore Burden graduated from Barry University (Miami Shores, Florida) with a Bachelors Degree in Nursing, and a Masters Degree in Criminal Justice from St. Thomas University (Miami Gardens, Florida).

She worked for 28 years with the City of Miami Police Department, in various units throughout the department, including undercover details. Frederica was also a calendar model for the Police Department. She has three (3) sons and currently works as an adjunct professor at Miami Dade College School of Justice.

Her debut novel Miami Beat: The Secret Society was published Spring 2018, followed by the sequel, Miami Beat II: Dilemmas in the Fall of 2018. Miami Beat III: Illusions is the final suspense novel in the trilogy series.

You can learn more about upcoming releases in the series at: www.FredericaBurden.com

Frederica Burden

www.ingramcontent.com/pod-product-compliance
Lightning Source LLC
Chambersburg PA
CBHW070019260626
47159CB00005B/1871